# Dora at Follyfoot

## MONICA DICKENS

ANDERSEN PRESS
LONDON

This edition first published in 2013 by
Andersen Press Limited
20 Vauxhall Bridge Road
London SW1V 2SA
www.andersenpress.co.uk

First published in 1972 by William Heinemann Ltd

British Library Cataloguing in Publication Data available.

ISBN 978 1 84939 680 6

Printed and bound in Great Britain by
CPI Group (UK) Ltd, Croydon, CR0 4YY

# Chapter 1

When Dora went into the stable yard after lunch, Slugger was sweeping.

'What's wrong, Slugger?'

Slugger Jones was a man of habit, whether indoors or outdoors, he slept after Sunday lunch, and he never swept the yard until after the evening feeds. Especially on a Sunday when visitors might come and scatter toffee papers, and hastily stamp out cigarettes when they saw Steve's notice:

EVERYTHING AT FOLLYFOOT BURNS, INCLUDING MY TEMPER

He had originally written, 'The Colonel's temper,' but had blacked that out and put 'my'.

'What's wrong, she wants to know.' Slugger swept

towards Dora's feet, and over them. 'Man doing a bit of honest work and she wants to know what's wrong.'

Dora looked over Willy's half door and made a face at the mule, who dozed with head down and ears lopped out from wall to wall. She felt like riding, but there was nothing much here that wasn't lame, stiff, blind, ancient, or pensioned off from work for the rest of its life. That was the only snag about a Home of Rest for Horses. Dora and Steve were always trying to sneak in a horse that was fit enough to ride.

Dora put a bridle on Willy and the old Army saddle that was the only one that fitted him, since his back had been permanently moulded by his days as an Army mule. When she brought him out, Slugger was leaning into the water trough to pull out the stopper.

'Where are you going?' His voice was a muffled echo inside the trough.

'Into the woods. I'm still trying to teach Willy to jump logs.'

'I wouldn't go there. Not in the woods I wouldn't, no.'

'Why?' What did he expect? Murderers? Madmen? The shadowed rides through the beechwoods were calm and safe as a cathedral.

'Ask a silly question, you get a silly answer.' Slugger was scrubbing a brush round the sides of the trough. 'You might miss someone.'

'What do you – oh, Slugger, was that what the telephone was? The Colonel?'

The Colonel, who owned Follyfoot Farm, had been in hospital for nearly two months. He was coming home at last.

Dora climbed on to the mule, slapped him down the shoulder with the reins because his armoured sides were impervious to legs, and rode out of the yard and down the road to be the first to greet the car.

At the crossroads she stopped and let Willy eat grass while she lolled in the uncomfortable saddle, and drifted into her fantasy world where she was brave in adventures and always knew the right things to say.

She heard the sports car on the hill. Even with Anna driving, the gearbox still made that unmistakable racket from losing battles with the Colonel. When the car stopped and he looked out with his lopsided smile, Dora hardly knew him. His face was thin and pale, his eyes and teeth too big. His hand on the edge of the car door was bony and white. He was still biting round his nails, but they were clean. At Follyfoot nobody's nails were ever completely clean, finger or toe.

'Hullo, Dora.'

'Hullo.' She pulled up Willy's head, not knowing what to say. *Are you all right?* Well, he must be, or he wouldn't come home. *Did it hurt?* Operations always hurt. *I'm glad you—*

Willy suddenly dropped his head and pulled her forward on to his bristly mane.

The Colonel laughed his old laugh that ended in a cough. Anna moved the car forward. Dora kicked Willy into his awkward canter and followed them home on the grass at the side of the road.

Callie, the Colonel's stepdaughter, was at the gate to open it, with his yellow mongrel dog in ecstasies, tail beating its sides. Slugger was in Wonderboy's loose box, pretending not to be excited. He came out with his terrible old woollen cap tipped over his faded-blue eyes, and the Colonel laid an arm across his shoulders.

'Good to be back, Slugger.'

'How's it gone then?'

'No picnic.'

'Teach you to stay away from that foul pipe.'

'It was the old war wound. The doctors say it was nothing to do with smoking.'

'That's what they say. I burned that old pipe.'

Anna wanted the Colonel to rest in the house, but he had to go all round the stables first, leaning on his stick, lamer than usual, and then out to the fields where some of the horses were grazing in the sweet spring day.

Fanny, the one-eyed old farm horse, trotted up to him. The Weaver lifted his head with his cracked trumpet call, and then went back to chewing the fence rail, weaving hypnotically from foot to foot. Lancelot, the oldest horse at the Farm, perhaps in the world, mumbled at the grass with his long yellow teeth and looked at the Colonel through his rickety back legs. Stroller, the brewery horse, plodded up and nosed into his jacket for sugar.

'He remembers which pocket.'

The Colonel had gone into and out of hospital wearing the patched tweed jacket with the poacher's pockets wide enough for a horse's nose.

In the jump field Callie was lungeing the yearling colt, Folly.

'Shaping up quite nicely.' The Colonel watched with his horsy look, eyes narrowed, a piece of hay in his mouth. Horses are always chewing grass or hay, and people who live with them catch the habit.

'What do you mean?' Callie bent as if she were going to pick up and throw a piece of earth, to make the colt trot out, head up, long legs straight, tail sailing. 'He's perfect!'

The Colonel laughed. 'Nothing changes, thank God. Where's Steve?'

'I think he's out with the horse box,' Dora said casually.

'What for?'

'Oh—' She stuck a piece of hay in her mouth too. 'To bring in a horse.'

'I thought the stable was full.'

'Well it is,' Dora said. 'But we found this horse, you see. The junk man died, and the old lady, she tried to keep it in the back garden, tied to the clothes line, and it's all thin and mangy like a worn old carpet, and so we...'

'And so they thought it was just what we needed to keep us busy in our spare time,' Slugger grumbled, leaning on the gate.

The Colonel laughed. 'Nothing changes.'

# Chapter 2

A few days after he came home from the hospital, the Colonel took Steve into his study for a long talk, and later he called in Dora.

He was sitting in the leather armchair with his feet on the fender in front of a bright fire. It was a good day, but he felt the cold more than he used to.

No one had used this room while he was away. It was so unnaturally tidy and clean that Dora stopped in the doorway to take off her boots.

'Come in, come in, there's a hell of a draught.'

She padded in her socks over the carpet that was as thin and worn as the old horse they had just rescued from the widow's clothes line. The horse's name was Flypaper, because it attracted flies. Dora was treating its moth-eaten patches with Slugger's salad oil.

'Sit down, Dora.'

She sat on the stool at the other side of the fireplace. The Colonel's hand wandered to the desk where his chewed pipe used to be, groped for a moment, then came back to his pocket and took out a paper bag.

'Have a peppermint.' He held the bag out to Dora and took one himself. 'Poor substitute for tobacco.' He stuck it in his lined cheek. 'But I'm trying.'

'Are you really all right?' The others pretended that he was the picture of health, but Dora always said what she thought. 'You look terrible.'

'Thanks.' He shifted the peppermint to the other cheek. 'I'd rather hear that than people telling me I look wonderful when I feel like death. It's going to be a long pull, I'm afraid.

'I've got to go abroad for a bit, Dora. Down to the South where it's warm and dry and there's nothing to do.' He made a face. 'I'd much rather be hanging round here in the rain and mud with the horses.'

'Don't worry about them,' Dora said quickly. 'We can manage.'

'Can you? I've been wondering if I ought to get someone in to run this place.'

'Oh no!' Dora stood up, her face stubborn. 'I couldn't work for anyone else.'

'What about Steve?'

'He's only a boy. I wouldn't let him boss me about.'

'All right,' the Colonel said. 'Give it a try as your own boss. I think you can cope, between you. If you get into a muddle with bills, my accountant will help you. Just be careful with money. Don't buy any horses. If you get a really needy case, of course take it in. Slugger will gripe, but fit it in somewhere. But no buying. Remember that Shire horse – the one you and Steve found at the Fair, and you sold the bicycle to get it?'

'And then found he was stolen anyway, and I had to give him back to the farmer.' Dora smiled, remembering the fat, sloppy horse with the curly moustache. 'Yes, I remember. It wasn't Steve. It was that boy Ron Stryker, and he'd stolen the bicycle.'

'That was when I fired him. Useless layabout. I never should have hired him. But you take what you can get these days. If you need any help—'

'We won't.'

'There's this chap I know. Bernard Fox. The one who has the big stable over the other side of the racecourse.'

'Where you can eat your dinner off the yard?' Dora had once sneaked a look round the grand Fox stables. 'It doesn't even smell of horse.'

'Well, we can't all manage that, Dora.'

As she stood with her arm on the mantelpiece among the Colonel's photographs and trophies and the silver model of his famous grey jumper, the fire brought out the stable essence of Dora's clothes.

'But Bernard says he'll be glad to help any time you need him.'

'We won't.'

'He may look in at the Farm some time. Be reasonably polite, will you?'

'I always am.'

'You do try.' The Colonel reached out and took her hand and squeezed it. 'Go ahead with the work then, Dora. It's all yours.'

When she went out, Steve was grooming a horse in the corner box. His head came over the door when he heard her feet on the cinder path.

'What did he say?' He had been waiting for her to come out of the house.

'He's got to go away.'

'I know.'

'He said about being careful with money. Not buying horses, and all that. What did he say to you?'

'That too, and – well, I'm more or less in charge.'

'Funny,' Dora said. 'That's what he said to me.'

*

'Who is in charge here?'

The woman who stormed into the yard was red in the face under a plastic rain bonnet. 'One of your ponies was out last night and walked all over my pansy bed.'

'The black and white beggar?' Slugger knew that Jock the Shetland was a magician pony who could squeeze through hedges and between fence rails, and undo bolts with his teeth.

'I didn't see the beastly thing.' She glared at Slugger from under the rain bonnet. 'Only its nasty little hoof marks, all over my pansy bed.'

'Spoil many plants?' Slugger asked.

'I haven't put any in yet. But that's not the point. I want something done.'

'I could send the boy up to rake over the bed,' Slugger said, and the red-faced woman pounced.

'Are you in charge?'

'Oh dear me, no. In charge, she says. Oh no, lady.' Slugger faded.

'Who *is* in charge here?'

'Not me.' Steve put on a dopey face.

'Not me.' Dora backed away.


But that evening when some visitors with children were going round the loose boxes, exclaiming and sighing and mooning over the old horses, the father asked Dora,

'Where's the boss then?' and she heard herself answering, 'Here. It's me.'

Then when she was with the children in the donkey's stable, lifting them onto his back, she heard the father say to Steve, 'Bit young, that girl, to run this place.'

And heard Steve laugh. 'She doesn't, actually. I do.'

# Chapter 3

Callie had refused to go abroad with her mother and the Colonel. She made the excuse of school.

'But there's only a few more weeks,' Anna said. 'You could join us at the villa then. You can swim down there, and sail and play tennis, and there are lots of young people your age.'

'I don't need young people my age. I need horses. And they need me.'

It was true. Callie was needed at Follyfoot. Steve and Dora and Slugger all worked extra hours, but the stable was full, and this was the time of year to mend fences and gates, to lime some of the fields, and prune dead branches out of trees and touch up peeling paint. Soon it would be time to get in the first crop of hay.

Dora sat up late at the Colonel's desk, falling asleep over bills and letters. Steve had taken over all the hoof care and the treatments for the unsound horses that the Colonel used to do. Slugger, who did the cooking as well as a thousand outside jobs, had not had a day off for weeks.

His sister came up to the Farm in her husband's dry-cleaning van to see if he was dead.

'Sorry to disappoint you, Ada.' Slugger set down a loaded wheelbarrow.

'An old man like you.' His sister clicked her loose teeth. 'You'll collapse on this job.'

'Then I'll be at the right place, won't I? They can put me out to grass with the old horses.'

Callie got up early to help in the stables before she caught the bus to school, and did mucking out instead of homework in the evenings.

Her teacher sent a note home. Dora answered it, signing herself 'Guardian', but the teacher threatened trouble if things did not improve, so Callie stayed away from school, to avoid the trouble.

An extremely polite man came to the Farm one afternoon and found Callie in the feed shed with a brush and a big pail of whitewash. She gave him an overall and another brush, and they worked together for the rest of the afternoon, and Slugger made tea for him before he left.

'Nice of him to help.' Steve came up from the bottom field with Dolly and the cart full of planks and saws and hammers. 'Friend of yours, Callie?'

'He was the attendance officer.'

Callie had to go back to school for the rest of the term, and she had to do her homework, to stop them writing to her mother and the Colonel.

There were two reasons why no one must write that sort of letter to Anna and the Colonel. One: Not to worry them. Two: If he thought Steve and Dora couldn't cope, the Colonel might bring in a manager to run Follyfoot. Or write to his friend Bernard Fox.

The Farm was sloppier than usual. The horses were content, but there was no time to do everything. The manure pile had not been spread, and was growing out alarmingly from the side of the barn. Straw was not stacked away in the Dutch barn. The horse box was still covered in mud from its last trip across a field. They did not want the grand stable keeper coming round with burnished boots and foxy face to match his name.

He did come. He came one morning when Steve and Dora were doing what Ron Stryker used to call 'taking five minutes'.

They were stretched out in the sun on two bales of straw, with Steve's radio going. The brown mare, Pussycat, who was wandering loose in the yard to pick up dropped hay, was thoughtfully licking the sole of Steve's shoe.

'Good morning, good morning.' He strode briskly into the yard, burnished Bernie Fox in tall polished boots and sharply-cut breeches, cap over his eyes, crisp ginger moustache at the ready. 'I hope I'm not interrupting your work.'

Steve jumped up and banged off the radio on a supersonic howl. Dora scrambled upright, pulling straw out of her hair. Old Puss leered with her lower lip hanging, and shambled stiffly away.

'Fox is the name. Bernard Fox. Good friend of the Colonel's. He asked me to keep an eye on things, so I thought I'd just look in as I was passing by.'

'How – how nice of you,' mumbled Dora. Steve said nothing. Boys never do, in a pinch. So Dora produced a few cracked words. 'Would you like to see round?'

Bernard Fox had already seen quite a lot in the few moments he had been in the yard. Straw bales in the corner instead of stacked away. A fork left in a loaded wheelbarrow. Muddy heads looking over doors, with burrs in their forelocks. Pussycat licking the door of the feed shed, the nearest she could get to oats.

'Better shut the yard gate while she's loose,' Mr Fox said.

'She never wanders away,' Dora told him.

'You can't assume anything with horses. They're unpredictable.'

'She knows when she's well off. She's gone far enough in her old life. A man was riding her from Scotland to London with a petition for the Queen. After a week, Puss lay down by the side of the road and wouldn't go any farther, so the man had to go on by train, and when he got to London the Queen was in Australia.'

Dora thought Bernard Fox would be interested, but he only said, 'I'd still like to see you shut the gate.'

He did not exactly order (he'd better not). He just stood there in the superb boots, with his foxy head cocked, confident of being obeyed.

Dora stamped off, muttering and growling. The gate had dropped, because the hinge was loose. With her back to Bernard Fox, she tried to latch it without him noticing that she had to lift it.

'Need some longer screws in that hinge, don't you?' he called out breezily.

He had several other breezy suggestions.

'Better get that muck pile shifted.' He looked round the side of the barn. 'Danger of spontaneous combustion. It's hot enough for mushrooms already, I see.'

'We're growing them to eat,' Steve invented. 'Organic gardening.'

They could not keep him out of the tack room.

Cobwebs. Mildewed leather. A bridle with a grass-stained bit hanging on the cleaning hook, as if that were enough to clean it.

'Colonel forgotten his Army training?'

'Of course not.' Dora was not going to have him criticising the Colonel. 'We've had no time to clean tack. Haven't got time to ride anyway.'

'And nothing much to sit on.' Bernard Fox's cold ginger eyes took in the few dusty old saddles, which were all they had.

'Bit risky.' He looked into the loose box where Stroller was keeping company with Prince, who had been turned out of his stable for Flypaper, whose mange might be catching.

'They get on all right.'

'Start a kicking match sooner or later. Why don't you turn 'em out?'

'It's going to rain.' Steve looked up at the low sky, which might let down water on Bernard's burnish at any moment. 'Stroller is rheumatic and Prince is coughing.'

'So will Stroller be, if you leave them together. Isn't there an isolation box?'

'Yes, the foaling stable. But Lancelot's in that.'

'Who's Lancelot?'

'The oldest horse in the world,' Dora said proudly.

Bernard Fox looked glumly over the door. Lancelot,

despite having a rack full of hay, was eating his bedding. He was the only horse who could manage to have both a pot belly and sticking out ribs. His wispy tail was scratched thin at the top. He had rubbed away half his mane under his favourite oak tree branch. His long teeth stuck out beyond his slack lips and his neck curved the wrong way, like a camel.

Bernard Fox looked at him for a long time, orange eyebrows raised, mouth pursed under the trim moustache. Lancelot looked back at him, his sparse lashes dropping over clouded eyes.

'Ought to have been put down long ago.'

'The Colonel doesn't believe in taking life.' Dora thought he couldn't know the Colonel very well, or he would be aware of that. 'Unless a horse is suffering.'

'I'm suffering just looking at him.'

'Lancelot is very content—' Dora began, but Bernard Fox had walked off to look over the gate of the jump field, where Folly and a few other horses were grazing. The gate was tied with a halter rope. One of the jumps was wrecked from Dora's efforts with the mule.

'Nice colt.' Even Bernard Fox could not find fault with Folly. 'Who's working with him?'

'Callie is beginning with the lunge and long rein. She's the Colonel's stepdaughter.'

'You'll be sending him to a trainer though?'

'I don't see why. Callie does very well for her age.'

'How old is she?'

'Twelve.'

'I see.'

He asked, 'How did the horse box get so filthy?' *Going over a ploughed field to rescue a fallen calf*, and, 'When are you going to get that stand of hay cut?' *When we have time*, and as he was crossing the yard to leave, 'What is that?'

It was Slugger, coming out of the back door in his long cooking apron and his woollen cap, waving and shouting, 'I did it! A loaf of bread – it rose! Come and get it before it falls down!'

'Would you like some home-made bread and butter?' Dora asked politely. Bernard Fox was so narrow and trim he did not look as if he got enough of things like that.

'Thanks, but I must get on. I've got an appointment. Big thoroughbred breeder from America.' *Who cares?* 'I've stayed longer than I should.' *Too true.* 'But I promised the Colonel I'd help, and I'm a man of my word.' *Too bad.* 'And help is what you youngsters need.'

Dora and Steve hated to be called youngsters. They were doing a grown-up job with grown-up responsibilities. They were paid. They were independent. They had both left home, more or less for good.

'We're all right.'

Instinctively they stood side by side, arms touching. They had fought and argued and annoyed each other many times since they were left on their own, but they were very close now, scenting the Fox as enemy.

'You need another stable hand.'

'We've got Slugger. And Callie.'

'Slugger is the one with the bread, I take it. And Callie is the twelve-year-old? I'll make some enquiries tomorrow and see if I can get hold of someone efficient. I'm sure the Colonel will agree.'

'Not to someone who treats horses like horses,' Dora said. Hard to explain what she meant – the caring, the understanding, the sharing of life between animal and man. Impossible to explain to Bernard Fox.

'Better than treating them like inmates of a cosy old folks' home,' he said. 'Good day to you, Miss Dorothy. Steven.' His hand went politely to his cap. Steve and Dora clicked heels and saluted, and Bernard turned on his burnished boots without a smile.

Dora's heels did not click very well. A puppy had eaten one of her shoes, and she was barefoot. As he passed her, Bernard Fox said out of the side of his mouth, 'You're asking for tetanus.'

# Chapter 4

Bernard Fox, a man of his word as he said, cabled for the Colonel's permission, and found a new stable hand within a few days.

It was a girl who used to work for him.

'Always these mucky girls,' Slugger and Steve grumbled to each other. 'Nothing but girls. Remember those two – Lily and Jane – used to squeal all the time and get their toes trodden on? Why can't we get a man round here? Nothing but sloppy, useless girls.'

Dora went on brushing mud off the white parts of the Appaloosa horse Spot (he never got mud on his brown patches where it wouldn't show), and pretended not to hear.

'If this new one wears tight purple trousers and dangly

earrings and calls me Daddy-O, I'm packing it in,' Slugger said.

'I'll go with you,' said Steve, 'if she paints her eyes like dart boards and wants to darn my socks.'

'He said "efficient".' Dora hung an arm over Spot's door to bang the mud out of the curry comb. 'He didn't say insane.'

Phyllis Weatherby, the efficient stable girl, was coming in two days' time. They pretended not to care, but they did work extra hard to spruce the place up so that she would know that this was how things were done at Follyfoot.

She was not on the afternoon bus with Callie.

'Relax, everybody.' Callie ran into the yard and spun her ugly school hat into a tree. 'Perhaps she won't come at all.'

Slugger went into the house to take off his boots and put his feet up. Steve and Dora settled down to play cards in the barn. Callie changed her hated school uniform for her beloved bleached jeans and took Folly for a walk to the village, showing him the world.

She was back quite soon in a car she had flagged down for a lift.

'He got away!' She panted into the barn. 'A car backfired and I couldn't hold him. He went off down the High Street with the rope trailing, knocked over a couple of bikes, went across the main road – cars swerving and screeching, it was awful – through a hedge and off across the fields, I've no idea where he's gone!' She sat down on a bale of hay, scattering the playing cards, and burst into tears.

'I'll get the truck. Dora, you take Hero and follow the colt. You can't miss those little tracks.'

Dora put a bridle on Hero, tried to vault on to him bareback, failed three times, and climbed on from the milestone mounting block. Steve was backing the truck out of the shed when Slugger ran shouting out of the house in his socks and his old indestructible Army vest and trousers.

'Folly's loose!'

Dora turned back. 'He's across the main road. That's where we're going.'

'He may be headed home. Mrs Ripley at the Three Horseshoes saw him run through her yard, "going like smoke", she said on the phone.'

Callie got into the truck. 'Hurry, Steve.'

'Better wait, if he's headed home.' Slugger put his hands on the door.

'How do we know?' Callie was anguished.

'Tearing round the roads won't help.'

'We've got to do something – let go!' She tried to pry his fingers from the edge of the door. She thumped them. She even bent down and bit the horny knuckles.

Slugger paid no more heed than if she were a fly. He had turned his head away to listen.

'Let go,' Callie pleaded. 'Oh hurry, Steve!'

But Steve had heard what Slugger had heard, and jumped out.

Specs, Folly's mother who had long ago seemed to forget the colt was hers, had heard it too. Her shaggy head was over the door, ears pricked, eyes staring out of the white circles round them. Her head swung up and she called, deep and throaty, as she had not called since Folly was a skittery foal straying too far from her in the field.

Other heads were coming out in a chorus of neighs, whinnies, grunts, and a donkey's ear-shattering bray. And then from beyond the hayfield at the bottom of the hill came the faint answer, high and shrill, unmistakably Folly.

Dora and Hero were off down the grass track, scrambling over the low bar in the gateway and down the side of the hay field to open the bottom gate for him. They came back together, Folly bounding and teasing, knocking up against Hero's stiff, steady trot, galloping off in a circle, snatching at the tall hay, running ahead with his tail up and his head down to buck and squeal.

At the bar, he stopped and sniffed. As Hero began to step carefully over, Folly took a flying leap and landed in front of him. Hero stumbled. Dora fell off. Hero recovered and trotted back to the yard without her.

At this moment, a car stopped in the road and a tall girl, in the sort of raincoat you see in photographs of sporting events, walked in.

Hero was wandering loose with one foot through his reins. Callie, with tear stains on her face, was chasing Folly round the yard, trying to grab the flying rope. Slugger was hobbling after her in his socks and khaki vest, swearing at the cobbles. Dora trailed in with mud on her behind.

'With all the practice you've had, you ought to be able to fall off on to your feet.' Steve laughed at her, and Dora wiped a muddy hand in his hair.

'Excuse me,' said the girl in the raincoat, 'is this Follyfoot Farm?'

'Foyft Fahm,' she said. She droned in her nose without opening her mouth, as if she couldn't spare the words.

She was no girl either, when you saw her close. Dry and leathery, she would never see thirty again, nor even thirty-five.

'Right,' she said, when she had introduced herself as Phlis Wethby. 'Right, let's get hold of that little clod.'

'I can't—' Callie was still breathlessly playing Tag, Folly's favourite game. Phyllis Weatherby strode over, and as Callie grabbed and he flicked away, she was there to catch him on the other side.

'Get'm off guard, right?'

Most of her sentences began and ended in 'right'.

'Right,' she'd say, 'we'll get the mucking out finished and this lot turned out and these other nags groomed before we break for lunch, right? Steven, you take the end stables and Dorothy can start down that side. Right, Slugger, there's all those cobwebs should have been got down from the beams years ago.'

'We keep 'em to catch flies.'

'Nonsense. Asking for coughs. Use the old birch broom, right?'

Dora followed Steve into the shed where the barrows and forks were kept.

'Right,' she droned between closed lips, 'you know what I think? She's come here to be boss, right?'

'Wrong.' Steve set his jaw.

But Phyllis Weatherby was hard to resist because, like Bernard Fox, she expected to be obeyed, which hypnotised you into obeying. Or she would tell you to do something you were just going to do anyway, so it put you under orders. She was hard to ridicule, because she had no sense of humour and couldn't tell the difference between a joke and an insult. When Slugger was driven to mutter, 'Oh, knock it off, you silly old cow,' she slapped poor Trotsky on his bony triangular rump and said, 'Right, he does look more like a cow than a horse.'

When Dora said, 'Right, Phyllis, it's your turn to load

the muck cart, right?' Phyllis answered, 'Right, you can take my turn while I soak that pony's leg, right, Dorothy?'

'The name is Dora, if you haven't washed your ears lately.'

'Short for Dorothy. Right?'

But she did her share of the work, you had to give her that. Rejecting the comfortable, shabby farmhouse because there were spiders in the bath and mice in the larder, she had taken a room at the Cross Keys Hotel in the village. But she was back at the Farm before anyone was up, throwing pebbles at the bedroom windows and clashing buckets fit to wake the dead, which Slugger sometimes wished he was when he woke and found that the nightmare of Phyllis Weatherby was true.

She brought her lunch from the hotel, because she couldn't get her tight-fisted lips round Slugger's doorstep sandwiches. She ate quickly, and jostled the others out of their usual hour of lazing in the sun, gossiping, dozing, reading, swilling mugs of the strong sugary tea which Phyllis prophesied would rot all their teeth.

This annoyed Slugger so much that one day he took out his teeth in his red bandana handkerchief and opened his mouth and said, 'Look, Phyll, it did.'

'You were right, right?' Dora grinned.

'All right, back to the mines.' Phyllis Weatherby dusted crumbs off her strong capable hands and stood up. 'Fooling about won't get the work done.'

She chivvied the old horses as much as the people who looked after them. Hero must be schooled, though he was long past it. The Weaver must wear a cribbing collar to break him of his habit of crib biting with his long yellow teeth on his manger or door – it didn't. Even Lancelot's senile dreams were disturbed. He did not care to go out in damp weather. You could open his door and he would just stand there, swinging his head like a hammer and watching the rain.

'Right, get a move on.' Phyllis pushed him towards the door with her shoulder. Though she was thin, she was sinewy and tough. 'Get out and get some exercise.'

'He's too stiff,' Dora said.

'If he's not sound, he shouldn't be kept alive.'

'That's what Bernard Fox said. Why does everyone want to put down poor old Lance?'

'If Mr Fox said it, it's right. He is a master horseman.'

'If you were the oldest horse in the world,' Dora hid her head against Lancelot's neck as he sagged at the edge of the orchard, too bored to eat grass, 'you wouldn't want a master horseman. You'd want a friend.'

'Well, he can't have it both ways,' Phyllis said offensively. 'He must either shape up or be put down.'

'That's not the point of Follyfoot,' Dora said into Lancelot's straggly mane.

'Right. I can see that.' Phyllis Weatherby began to shake up bedding, hissing to herself as if she were a horse.

How were they going to get rid of her?

# Chapter 5

Quite a lot of their time was spent discussing how this could be done without trouble. Phyllis Weatherby was in touch with Bernard Fox. He would hear from her about trouble, and report it to the Colonel.

How were they going to get rid of her?

One Sunday when Steve had gone to see his mother, and Callie and Dora wanted to try and make a dress, Phyllis insisted on taking them to a horse show to see what riding was.

'We know what riding is,' Callie objected. 'We just don't happen to have anything much to ride.'

'If some of these old horses had been kept working,' said Phyllis, to whom a horse was a vehicle, 'they wouldn't have stiffened up, right?'

The show was quite large and smart, with a lot of teenage girls on expensive horses with jockey caps tipped over their noses and a blasé air of having seen it all before. Which they had, because they had been going to shows ever since their ambitious mothers stuck them on a pedigree Shetland in the Leading Rein class before they could walk.

They all rode beautifully and their horses were perfectly trained. Phyllis Weatherby thought this should be inspiring, but Dora and Callie found it rather depressing.

'Push-button ponies,' Callie said, to cover her jealousy of the splendid well-schooled ponies trotting round the ring in the Under 12.2 Hands class. 'What's the fun of that?'

'More fun than something that either won't go or runs away.' Phyllis stood at the rails with a know-all face, wearing jodhpurs to look like an exhibitor.

'If you're referring to the day Willie wouldn't move and Stroller took Steve into the pond—' Dora began, but Phyllis was laughing at something in the ring, high in her nose, an unusual sound. She didn't laugh much, and when she did it was at, not with, people.

'Look at that,' she jeered. 'If that's a push-button pony, someone's pushing the wrong button, right?'

Out among the show ponies and the snobby little girls with hard eyes, someone had mistakenly sent a long-legged boy, top heavy on a tiny dun Shetland. His feet were almost on the ground. When they cantered, he had to lean back to keep his balance. The little pony was slower than the others. They passed it or bumped into it, the snobby little girls swearing at it from the sides of their mouths without losing their smug, professional faces. One of them flicked at the Shetland with a whip as she went by. It swerved, and the boy lost his balance. His jockey cap, which was too big for him, tipped over his eyes.

He pushed it back vaguely and cantered on. He was a thin, dreamy-looking boy, apparently unaware that he was a spectacle.

'Somebody ought to tell him.' Dora could hardly look. 'It's not fair.'

'Let him make an ass of himself.' Phyllis Weatherby laughed in her nose again. 'Serves him right.'

'I meant not fair to the pony. He's much too big for it.'

'A Shetland can carry twelve stone.' Phyllis and Dora had got into the habit of always arguing. Either of them would say black was white to contradict the other.

The rosettes were awarded. Four smug faces rode out of the ring, and ten disgruntled ones, plus the dreamy boy who did not seem to have noticed defeat. Outside the gate, his parents, plump and tweedy, received him and the pony with hugs and lumps of sugar, and the father took several pictures, getting in the way of the next class going into the ring.

'Let's go and tell them,' Callie urged Dora.

'Mind your own business,' Phyllis said. But when she was watching the next class, with comments to show she knew a thing or two: 'Snappy little roan...pulls like a train...overflexed, etc., etc.,' they slipped away.

Walking over to the horse box lines, Dora asked Callie, 'What shall we say?'

'He's too big for the pony. It's cruel.'

'But they look as if they were just stupid, not cruel.'

'Stupidity is cruelty.' Callie echoed the Colonel. 'People who don't know anything about horses shouldn't be allowed to keep them.'

But this was one of the most difficult things about being in the business of animal rescue. Easy to attack deliberately cruel owners who beat or starved their horses, or drove old crocks into the ground. Much harder to tell kind, sentimental fools that their 'pet' was suffering through their ignorance.

It was too late anyway to tell the plump tweed-suited people anything. Among the smartly-painted horse boxes and trailers was a red minibus. As Dora and Callie came up they saw it move away, the father driving, the mother beside him in her mauve tweed hat to match her suit, and the dreamy boy in the back with the dun pony.

They must have lifted it in, and it was small enough to stand between the seats, like a dog.

'Let's follow them.'

Phyllis had come after Dora and Callie to see what they were up to. She behaved like their keeper, in or out of the stable.

'Want a laugh?' They pointed to the minibus turning out of the gates of the showground. 'Guess what's in that?'

'What?'

'Get the car and we'll show you. Let's follow them.'

They caught up with the red bus. The dun pony's head was sticking out of the back window, so Phyllis had her laugh. She passed the bus, hooted, then slowed down to let it pass her, so she could get another laugh. The boy's face was alongside the pony's, his fair hair blowing with its mane. Callie waved at him and grinned, so that he would not think they were making fun of him, and he waved back.

In a suburban road of neat houses with trimmed lawns and clipped hedges, the red bus stopped at a white stucco house called The Firs, and turned up the drive. Phyllis slowed for a last look.

'I'm going to tell them now.' Dora turned the handle of the car door.

'You can't do that.' Phyllis moved forward as the door opened. Dora and Callie fell out, and she drove away without them. Leaning back to pull the door shut, she shouted, 'All right, walk home, right?'

They picked themselves up from the drive, picked gravel out of the palms of their hands and followed the bus.

# Chapter 6

There was a sign on the side of the red minibus, 'J. R. Bunker Ltd. Builders and Decorators.'

'We saw your pony at the show,' Dora said. 'Can we have another look at it?'

'Help yourself.' Mr Bunker was headed for the house. 'Mind she doesn't bite.'

The dun pony had been put into a garden shed, which she shared with flower pots and spades and more dangerous things like scythes and empty bottles. There was no window and no half door. She stood in the dark, and when Dora opened the door, she nipped out under her arm and off into the garden.

Callie ran to catch her.

'Don't worry,' Mrs Bunker said. 'She always does that.

My little lawn mower, I call her.'

Callie was tugging at the pony's mane, but she could not move her, nor get her head up from the turf.

'She'll only come if you hold sugar in front of her,' Mrs Bunker said. 'Or an ice-cream cornet. She loves chocolate ices, anything sweet. That's why we call her Lollipop.'

'Is it good for her?' A question was more tactful than a statement.

'Good heavens, I don't know.' Mrs Bunker turned on Dora, her round amber eyes like glass beads without much behind them. 'But I'm so fond of dumb animals, you see, I can't deny them what they want.'

'That's not being kind,' Dora said bluntly, her tactfulness used up. 'That's being foolish. Did you give your son everything he wanted when he was a baby?'

'Yes, of course.' The round eyes were surprised at the question. 'He's our only child, you see.'

The dreamy boy was sitting on a wall, kicking the heels of his riding boots and humming to himself. His pony had not been fed or watered. His saddle was on the ground where he had dropped it. His bridle hung upside down on the branch of a tree.

'He's too big for Lollipop.' Callie had her belt round the neck of the dun pony, whose ears did not reach her shoulder.

'I know, isn't it absurd? But all the children round here go to the shows, so Jim does too, though he never wins, because the judges are crooked. The whole thing is rigged.'

'It's because he's too big for the pony,' Callie repeated. 'Should we get another one?'

'Oh no!' Dora burst out. 'I mean, you'd have to build a proper stable, wouldn't you, and find out how to take care of it. There's a lot more to keeping a horse than sugar and chocolate cornets.'

'We didn't know.' Mrs Bunker twisted her plump ringed hands. 'Everyone seems to have a pony. We didn't know it was all that difficult. How do you girls know so much?'

'We work at Follyfoot Farm,' Dora said. 'The Home of Rest for Horses.'

Mrs Bunker's eyes misted over at once. Always a bad sign when people began to blubber at the mere idea of an old horse. 'Ah, the dear patient beasts. I read a piece in the papers about the horse you rescued with the broken jaw. I couldn't do that kind of work. I'm too sensitive. I can't stand suffering.'

'You're making Lollipop suffer,' Callie said.

Mrs Bunker's hands went to her mouth. 'Oh, but we didn't know. We didn't know.'

'Famous last words,' Dora muttered.

'Perhaps we should get rid of her – send her to the auction sales.'

'I wouldn't. You don't know who'll buy her. Find her a good home.'

'It would break Jim's heart.'

'No it wouldn't, Mum, honest.' The boy, who had not spoken a word so far, slid down from the wall and came over. 'I don't care whether I ride or not, honest I don't.'

'Oh, but you do! Everybody rides. The Maxwell children ride, and the Browns, and all Sir Arthur's kiddies up at the Manor. All the children round here have ponies, and all those who don't wish they had.'

'They can have Lollipop then.' Jim kicked a stone along the path, went after it and kicked it again, scuffing the toe of his riding boot, trying to kick it into a drain.

'We could look for a home for her,' Callie said.

'But I'd be so sad. How could I face those trusting eyes?'

'We could have her at the Farm till we—'

Dora trod on Callie's toe. 'No more horses, the Colonel said,' she hissed.

'He said not to buy any.' Callie turned back to Mrs Bunker. 'Till we find a good home.'

Mrs Bunker went to ask her husband who, for all his proud photographing, seemed glad to have Lollipop off his hands. He came out at once and put her into the bus before they could change their minds. Callie and Dora sat at the back with the pony. Jim did not come. He sat on one of the gateposts with a magazine, waved to Lollipop and went back at once to the magazine.

Halfway up the hill, a light truck came up behind them. Dora and the pony happened to look out of the window together, and the truck swerved and nearly went into a tree. It was Steve.

He recovered and passed them, tapping his head to show they were mad. At the gate of the Farm, he opened the door of the bus, and the pony hopped neatly down.

'What the—?'

'Just for a short time,' Dora told him in the soothing voice she used on the Colonel.

'We agreed not to take in anything unless we both—'

'Case of desperate need,' Dora whispered. 'Extreme brutality.'

Steve scratched his head. The amiable parents in the minibus did not look like extreme brutes.

Phyllis Weatherby was waiting too, in the entrance to the stable yard.

'How dare you!' She was red in the face, trying to shout through closed lips. 'How dare you!'

'These nice young people are going to find a home for dear little Lollipop.' Mrs Bunker leaned out of the bus window, all smiles and beads.

'Not here, they aren't,' Phyllis Weatherby said rudely.

Mr Bunker, fearing a hitch, put the bus into gear and moved off before Phyllis could put the pony back in.

'Wait!' she called, and ran after them in her classy corduroys, knock-kneed instead of bow-legged, which she should be at her age if she was really as horsy as she said. 'Come back!'

The bus gathered speed. She stopped and shook her fist. Mrs Bunker pretended she thought she was waving, and waved back gaily out of the window.

Phyllis Weatherby was so angry she was almost in tears, Dora was almost sorry for her.

'I told you not to interfere with that pony. I told you!'

'So what?'

'You're not the boss.' Steve had to be on Dora's side, against Phyllis.

'Mr Fox said—'

'Mr Fox, Mr Fox. He's not the boss either.'

'I'm going to tell him.'

'Tell away.' Steve laughed. If he had not been bigger than Phyllis, she would have hit him.

'Where are you going with that pony?' She picked on Callie, who was smaller. 'There's no stable room, and if you put it out, the others will kick its stupid head in.'

'I'm not going to.' Callie was walking the little pony like a dog on a lead.

'Take it back,' Phyllis Weatherby ordered. 'It's a long walk, but serve you right. Take it back.'

She stormed into Flypaper's stable and began ferociously mucking out, swearing at the amiable horse to 'Move over! Get up, damn you!' Flypaper stood by the end wall and looked at her with hurt, astonished eyes.

Callie tied the pony to a stake on what had been a lawn by the house when anyone had time to keep a lawn.

Dora went to get her jacket out of Phyllis Weatherby's car. Steve called her urgently to help with Lancelot, who had sagged down to roll and couldn't get up, and she ran, leaving the car door open.

This is what they pieced together afterwards:

Callie was famous for rotten knots. Lollipop, who was a clever little pony, must have untied the rope with her teeth, wandered away and got into the car, reminded of her own minibus. When Phyllis left, still blindly furious, she banged shut the door and did not find out until she slammed on the brakes at the Cross Keys Hotel and a soft nose bumped the back of her neck, that she had a tiny pony sitting on the floor of her car.

'Carried on shouting,' the hotel manager told Dora on the telephone. 'She turns the pony loose, goes straight upstairs and packs her bags and takes off. "Send the bill to the Farm," she says.'

'Oh Lord.'

'It's not so much that, since I trust the Colonel. But the pony is in my wife's kitchen garden. She's holding it off her lettuce seedlings with a rake.'

Dora went on her bicycle to fetch Lollipop, and led her home, trotting by the back wheel. A car with a silver thoroughbred on the radiator slowed alongside.

'Phyllis Weatherby stopped by my place on her way home,' Bernard Fox said. 'Had some trouble?'

'Oh no, no trouble at all.' Dora wobbled. It is hard to ride a bicycle slowly and talk to someone in a car without bashing into it or falling off, especially when you are leading a pony.

'Phyllis was very upset.'

'She was tired. Working too hard.'

'Some strange story about someone putting a horse in her car...'

'There you are, you see. Hallucinations from overwork.'

'It will be hard to find another worker like that.'

'Don't bother.' Dora put the hand with the leading rein on to the handlebar and steadied herself with her other hand on his car. 'We've got someone.'

'Have you really?'

Dora nodded. Not quite as big a lie without speech.

'I'll stop in and have a chat with them.'

'They're not there yet. They should be coming in a few days.'

'If they don't, I'll find you someone else.'

Dora let go the car as he drove on, wobbled sideways, and the Shetland pony bit her on the ankle.

# Chapter 7

They sat up late that evening, laughing about Lollipop in the back seat, and worrying about Bernard Fox.

'If we don't find another stable hand,' Dora was lying on the floor with the Colonel's yellow mongrel, 'burnished Bernie will.'

'And it could be worse than Phyllis.'

'Impossible.' Slugger had disliked Phyllis from the first day, when she told him to put his hands under the tap before he went to work in the stable. 'Before!' He was still stewing over it. '"Carrying germs of disease," she says. So I says to her, "If there's any disease round here, it's in your head."'

'You didn't,' Callie said.

'I should have. The next one we get, I'm going to tell 'em first day who's boss here.'

'Who is?'

'Me.' Slugger thumped his chest into a hacking cough.

'Who are we going to get? The Colonel tried all the agencies when Ron Stryker left, and there wasn't anyone who knew one end of a horse from the other.'

'Easy,' Slugger said. 'One end bites and the other kicks.'

'We'll have to try.' Steve tipped back his chair. 'Oh Lord.' He let it down with a crash. 'Suppose Bernard Fox persuades Phyllis to come back?'

'She was in love with him,' Callie said sombrely. 'The master horseman.'


With no Phyllis Weatherby to clash buckets and throw stones at windows, they all slept late. Callie missed the bus for school, so Steve took her down in the truck and went on into Town to go round the employment agencies.

Dora went out to start feeds. She whistled her way round the stables, glad to be on her own, although there was so much work to do. It was easier to start a day by yourself, and work your way gradually into sharing it with other people.

Horses, that was different. It was biologically impossible for a horse to get on your nerves. They were always glad to see you, each one greeting you in its own way. Wonderboy with a high neigh. Ginger with a low whinny. The Weaver with a hoof tattoo on his door.

Stroller nodding his head up and down. Hero standing diagonally across his box with his nose in the manger to make sure you knew where to put the feed.

Prince, who would never trust people again, stood at the back of his box, flicking his ears. Dora spoke to him and went in quietly. He was still nervous, even with months of gentle handling, after his terrible experience at the brutal hands of the Night Riders. His mouth was permanently ruined by the crude wire bit. Dora was tipping the soft mash of bran and crushed oats and molasses into the manger when a shattering roar made the horse jump, and tread on her toe.

It is the hardest thing in the world to get a horse off your toe. Pushing her shoulder against his, Dora finally managed to get Prince off her poor big toe, which was already permanently bruised and blue, the trademark of a horse keeper.

She limped angrily out to see who was insane enough to ride a motorcycle into a farm full of horses.

She might have known. Strolling across the yard, lighting a cigarette and throwing down the burning match, his long red hair tangled on the shoulders of a fringed purple jacket—

'Ron. Ron Stryker. I might have known.'

'Missed me, eh? Knew you would. So I took pity on you and came back to work.'

'The Colonel's not here.'

'Oh, he'll be glad. Always liked me, did the Colonel.'

'Is that why he fired you?'

'Just a temporary misunderstanding, my dear.' Ron held out his hand as if to shake Dora's hand, then quickly grabbed her arm and kissed her.

Dora hated being kissed. Or did she? She was never quite sure. But she knew she hated being kissed by Ron Stryker. She wiped the back of her hand across her mouth, and Ron picked up the bucket and went into the feed shed and began to measure out oats and horse nuts, just as if he had never been away.

Dora went to tell Slugger. 'How are we going to get rid of him?'

'Why try?' Slugger had lost many battles with this cocky, tricky boy. 'If we've got to have another stable hand, you know what they say: Better the devil you know... Find out where he's been working, and we'll send for references.'

'Well, I'll tell you.' Ron leaned on a pitchfork, and slid his eyes sideways in the way Dora knew so well when he was thinking up a good fable. 'I been working for these blokes, name of Nicholson, see? Lovely people. Very classy. Head groom, I was.'

'Come off it, Ron.'

'Well, I mean, until we had the spot of trouble.'

'Get the sack again?'

'No, dear, I resigned. We parted like gentlemen, Mr Nicholson and me.'

'Then he won't mind if Steve or I write for a reference?'

'Well, of course he won't mind.' Ron's eyes slid off in the other direction. 'But why bother? The Colonel knows me. Why waste a stamp?'

When Slugger came out and saw the shaggy red head appear over a stable door, he said, 'I thought it couldn't be worse than Phyllis Weatherby, but it is.'

'Kind of you to say so.' Ron grinned with his chin on the door like a puppet.

'Steve phoned,' Slugger told Dora. 'The truck packed up in Middlebrough, and he's leaving it at a garage there. He never got to Town. I told him our troubles was over now that Superman was back on the job, so he said for Ron to go and fetch him home on the back of the bike.'

'There, you see.' Ron came out of the stable, wiping his hands on his tight jeans. 'You do need me. How do, General?' He shook hands with Slugger, and Slugger yelled and pulled his hand away from the trick crusher handshake.

# Chapter 8

Dora wrote to the Colonel, and he wrote back with a sigh in his handwriting:

'*All right. Keep Ron Stryker if you can stand him. At least he knows the job. Anna says lock away the silver. P.S. What happened to the girl Bernard Fox found?*'

'Better answer that bit right away,' Steve said, 'before be hears from Bernie.'

'You answer.'

'You'll make it sound better.'

Steve hated writing letters. His childhood had been a strange one, with no love and not much schooling. So Dora banged out a story on the typewriter in the study.

It began: '*There was this little tiny pony, you see...*' and ended up: '*I know it was bad luck on poor old*

*Phyllis, but we laughed till we fell down and you would have too.'*

Steve offered to fetch Ron's trunk, his guitar, his stereo set, his transistor, his cowboy boots and his collection of comic papers from the Nicholsons' where he had lived.

'The truck won't be ready till next week, but we can take the horse box. More room for all the loot you've probably knocked off. Come on, Ron.'

'I haven't the time to come with you.' Ron picked up a broom and started to sweep.

'Parted like gentlemen.' Dora laughed. 'Are you scared Mr Nicholson will shoot you on sight?'

'Lovely people.' Ron did not answer awkward questions. 'Salt of the earth.'

Dora went with Steve in the front of the horse box, following the directions Ron had written:

*Left at the boozer, fork right past that crummy place where they make pies out of dead cats, over the crossroads where the bus crashed and they had to cut the people out with a blow torch, straight through that town where the bloke murdered his wife, right at the boozer, left at the next boozer, and down Suicide Hill, you can't miss it.*

The 'lovely people' turned out to be horse dealers. It was a huge stable with about fifty horses in loose boxes, stalls and fenced yards, the sort of come-and-go place where horseflesh is just that – flesh, not soul – and represents only money.

Mrs Nicholson was in the large tack room, bullying two girls who were cleaning bridles. She was a beefy woman with muscles like a man and cropped grey hair round a shiny red face.

'Ronald Stryker!' She let out a bellow that set the curb chains jingling. 'I told that rotten little creep if he didn't get out of the county, I'd set the police on him.'

'What did he do?' Dora asked.

'It was what he didn't do,' Mrs Nicholson said darkly. 'Such as work. Keeping his fingers off other people's property. Following orders. Watching his mouth. Want any more?'

'We just came for his things.'

'You'll have to ask my husband.' Mrs Nicholson picked up two heavy saddles together and slung them with ease on to a high rack. 'I threw the junk out of the staff cottage and he put it somewhere. Out in the rain, I hope.'

Mr Nicholson was roughly the same shape as his wife, and the same colour, and made the same kind of loud noises.

'Stryker!' His veined red face grew purple. His bull neck swelled over the collar of his rat-catcher shirt. 'You friends of his?'

Dora nodded. Ron was right. Waste of a stamp to write for a reference.

'Bad luck on you. His stuff is in the shed out there with the tractor. If he hadn't sent for it, I was going to put it on the dustcart tomorrow.'

They found the tin trunk (heavy as lead, what on earth was in it?) and the guitar and the transistor and stereo and a strange garment like a military greatcoat from the First World War with holes where the buttons and badges used to be. They put it all into one side of the horse box, and were shutting up the ramp when a familiar red minibus pulled up in front of the long stable building.

Mrs Bunker waved to Steve and Dora, then dropped her hand uncertainly. 'I do know you, don't I? Oh yes, of course, Lollipop. How is the darling pony?'

'Eating,' Dora said. 'A nice family came to see her yesterday. They may take her.'

'It will break Jim's heart.'

'No, it won't, Mum,' he reminded her.

'Oh no, of course, because you'll have your new pet. We're here to look at a larger pony.' Mrs Bunker was dressed too smartly, everything matching, not quite right for the country.

'I thought you were giving up horses,' Dora said.

'We were, but people were quite surprised to hear that Jim didn't ride any more. I met Mrs Hatch who runs the

Pony Club camp, and when she heard that Jim wouldn't be camping this year, she was quite disappointed. Then Mr Bunker was up to look at the roof at Broadlands. You know, that huge old place where poor Mr Wheeler lives by himself since he lost his wife. My husband does all his work. And the old gentleman asks him, "How's Lollipop?" He takes such an interest in the young people. When he heard she was too small for Jim, he supposed we'd get something larger. So when Mr Bunker went up to supervise his men who are building the squash court up at the Manor, Sir Arthur told him this would be the best place to look.'

'But you've got no stable.' Dora's heart sank. A Shetland in that cluttered shed was bad enough. A large pony would be disaster.

'Oh yes. Mr Bunker has put up one of those nice pre-fabs.'

Dora's heart sank lower. They might acquire a large pony and a nice pre-fab stable, but where were they going to get sense?

'Where's Jim?' Mr Bunker, who was also dressed rather too smartly, came out of the stables brushing hay off the trousers of his unsuitable suit.

His wife looked round. 'He's wandered off somewhere.'

'Well, you come along, Marion. They have several fine

animals here, and the daughter is going to show them. Why don't you come with us?' he asked Steve and Dora. 'You know more than we do.'

He looked down and picked another piece of hay off his suit. Mrs Bunker was easy to understand. Foolish. Mr Bunker was more complicated. Hard to tell how shrewd he was, or whether he was laughing at you.

Steve and Dora put a piece of hay in their mouths and followed him through the stables to a schooling ring on the other side, where a girl the same shape as the Nicholsons, but smaller, was leading out a nervy black pony.

She had a hard-boiled face and a tough, professional manner. She mounted, adjusted her stirrups, checked the girth, muttered to the restless pony, and looked at her father for instructions.

'Trot him out a bit, Chip.' He leaned on the rail with his cap over his eyes and his legs crossed. 'Chip off the old block, she is.' He watched her trot the black pony smoothly round the track, perfectly flexed, stepping out. 'Extend the trot!' Chip obeyed, without appearing to move her legs or hands. 'It's all there under you,' Mr Nicholson said to the Bunkers, who hadn't a clue what he meant. 'You can't fault him. Right, Chip – walk. Then canter him a figure eight.' All his orders were bellowed, as if Chip were deaf or at the other end of a football field.

The showy black pony made impeccable figure-of-eights, cantering very slow and supple, performing a flying change of leads without breaking the rhythm.

'Win anywhere with that one,' Mr Nicholson said. 'Always in the money.'

Chip had stopped in front of them, as if they were judges at a horse show, the black pony standing out well, head up, ears forward. Mrs Bunker's amber eyes grew dreamy, imagining Jim in that saddle with the red rosette on his bridle.

Dora read her thoughts. 'But Jim could never ride that pony,' she said tactlessly, and realised that the thin pale boy had materialised at her side. Or could you, Jim?'

'I don't know.' He was a very negative boy, half in the world, half in his own dream world.

'Looks quiet enough to me,' his father said.

'That's because that girl knows how to ride it.'

'So will young Jim. He's taking lessons,' Mrs Bunker said. 'Sir Arthur suggested it, and told us the best instructor to go to.'

'But does he really want a show pony?'

On the other side of Dora, Steve nudged her and muttered, 'Shut up. It's their business.'

'That pony's hotter than it looks. The child will get killed.'

'No, I won't,' Jim said placidly.

'You like the pony, young man?' Mr Nicholson looked down at him from under his cap.

Jim shrugged his shoulders.

'He likes it,' the mother said. 'What's its name?'

'What's his name, Chip?' The dealer did not know the name of horses who passed through his hands, without looking at his records.

'Dark Song.'

'Oh, that's a lovely name.' Mrs Bunker's eyes shone. 'I think we should buy it, James.'

'How much?'

In the etiquette of horse trading, it was much too soon to mention money. Mr Nicholson cleared his throat and recrossed his legs the other way. 'I'll make you a price.'

'How much?' repeated Mr Bunker, forging on like one of his own bulldozers.

'Five hundred to you.'

'Too much.'

'It's a steal.' Mr Nicholson looked outraged, trying to embarrass the Bunkers. 'He's worth far more than that, but I like to send my customers away happy. Then they come back.'

'Oh, we wouldn't come back, I don't think,' Mrs Bunker said. 'If we bought that pretty pony, we wouldn't need another.'

'It's too much.' Her husband was coming out of this more strongly than she was. 'Show us something else.'

Chip, who had been sitting impassively in the saddle, staring straight ahead, raised one sandy eyebrow and rode out of the ring.

She came back with a chunky little chestnut, white socks, white blaze, picking up his feet, very showy. She trotted and cantered him, and when her father shouted, 'Pop him over some fences!' she and the pony soared over jumps of bloodcurdling height without either of them turning a hair.

'Do you think Jim could learn to ride like that?' Mrs Bunker's eyes were again dreaming of her son sailing over fences in an arena where the crowd roared.

'On that pony, he could,' said Mr Nicholson (child murderer). 'Quiet as a baby. Anyone could ride him.'

'He was pulling all the way.' Dora had to say it.

'Mouth like velvet.' Mr Nicholson shot her a look. 'You could ride him to church.' He had all the horse-trading clichés. 'What do you say, young man?' He clapped a heavy hand on Jim's narrow shoulder.

Jim shifted a sweet to the other side of his mouth. 'I don't really care for jumping, thank you,' he said politely.

'OK, Chip. Get that bay pony out here.'

A stable boy was standing by the gate of the ring, holding a pony which was probably the one they had planned to sell to the Bunkers. The other two were window dressing. It was a plain but pleasant-looking bright bay. It moved rather lifelessly with Chip, who looked bored, hopped neatly enough over two small jumps, stopped, stood still.

'Perfect picture of a child's hunter,' Mr Nicholson said, though it did not look as if it had enough energy to keep up with hounds for long. 'Tailor-made for you. Willing and wise. Safe as a rock. Look at him stand. Grow barnacles, that one would, before he'd move on without command.'

'You think that's the one we should buy?' Mrs Bunker asked naïvely.

'If you ask my advice, Madam, I'll give it to you,' Mr Nicholson said, as if he did not dish out advice all day long whether anyone asked for it or not. 'You'll not find a pony of this quality, if you—'

'How much?' Mr Bunker interrupted.

The dealer named a price that was less than the black or the chestnut, but far too much for this rather ordinary pony whose quality, if he had any, was not in his looks.

But Mrs Bunker was prodding her husband with a finger in a white glove and hissing, 'Let's!'

'You like it, son?'

'He loves it,' Jim's mother said. 'What's its name?'

'What's his name, Chip?'

The girl shrugged. She got off and led the pony away, as if she were sick of riding it.

'His name is Barney,' Jim said, more positively than usual.

'Why, dear?'

'Grow barnacles, he said.' Jim only listened to scraps of conversation. 'Barnacle Bill.'

'What do you think?' Mrs Bunker asked Steve and Dora.

'There's something not quite right about him.' Mr Nicholson had not moved away, so Dora had to say it in front of him.

'You should get him vetted,' Steve said. 'He looks a bit off.'

'The vet's just seen him,' Mr Nicholson cut in. 'Touch of shipping fever. We've only had him down from Scotland a few days. They always get a touch of that, didn't you know?'

'No,' Steve said, meaning: They don't always get shipping fever; but Mr Nicholson took it to mean that he didn't know, and said tartly, 'You kids don't know everything.'

'Will he fit in the bus?' Mrs Bunker asked.

'Hardly, Madam.' How could he sell a perfectly good pony – any pony – to people who so obviously knew nothing? 'But I'll tell you what I'll do for you. I'll get one of my men to hitch up the trailer and run him over to your place this afternoon, so your boy—'

'How much extra?'

Mr Nicholson named a figure that was roughly twice the fair price for transporting a horse that distance. Then his thick hands clenched and the cords of his neck stood out as Dora told the Bunkers cheerfully, 'We've got our horse box here, and we have to go right by your place. We'll bring him.'

There was something a little funny about the pony. Something about the expression of his eyes – *What was it?*

He was very stubborn. When Chip led him up to the horse box, he stopped dead at the foot of the ramp, with his head stuck out and his jaw set against the pull of the halter rope. Mr Nicholson picked up a handful of gravel and threw it. He shouted, he hit the pony with a whip, he tried to pull it in with a long rope round the quarters. He finally hit it with a short plank of wood and called it an obstinate swine. Chip flung the halter rope over the pony's neck and went away.

Mrs Bunker began to wring her hands. Jim had wandered away. Steve, who had been standing watching with his hands in his pockets, said, 'Can I try?'

'He's all yours.' Mr Nicholson walked off, so unfortunately he didn't see Steve speak to the pony and stroke it and get it to relax. Then he held it while Dora lifted a front foot and set it on the ramp. As the pony relaxed more, she was able to put the other foot on. Barnacle Bill stayed like that for a while, with his eyes half closed, then he sighed, and walked quietly into the horse box.

# Chapter 9

Ron Stryker was as lazy and dodgy as ever. He had to be watched since he did not instinctively put the horses before himself, as the others did.

Steve came in to supper one evening and found him with his face already in a bowl of Slugger's pea soup that was almost thick enough to eat with a knife and fork.

'I thought you'd done the buckets,' Steve said. 'You didn't give Ranger any water.'

Ron shrugged. 'That's his problem.'

'Get on out there and see to it.' Slugger threatened him with the carving knife.

'*I* did.' Steve sat down with a sigh.

'Don't worry, Slug,' Ron said soothingly, through soup. 'There's always some mug to do it.'

But he was an extra pair of hands, and they were getting back to their old routine, and the farm was straightening up.

'Burnished Bernie can come any time he likes.' Dora looked round the tidy yard, barrows lined up, tools hanging in place, manure heap cleared, and the clatter of Mr Beckett's mower coming up like evening insects from the hay field. 'Perhaps we should invite him before something goes wrong.'

'Never invite trouble.' Slugger shook his head.

'He's sure to come and check on Ron.'

'He'd better come on me day off,' Ron said from the roof of the donkey stable where he was plucking odd chords out of his guitar, 'for he won't like what he sees.'

'Why don't you change the image then?' Dora looked up, and he threw a piece of loose tile at her.

'Can't,' he said. 'I was borned like this.'

'With long red hair and jeans that stand up by themselves?'

'Yus.'

Callie stayed home from school and they worked all next day raking the cut hay into windrows. By the time they had done the evening stable work, everyone was exhausted. But Dora was restless. Ever since they had put

Barney into the Bunkers' clean, roomy loose box, sweet with the tang of new wood, she had been worried.

'It's not your business,' Steve said when she worried aloud.

But Dora went on worrying. Every horse was her business. She hated politics, but the only reason she would like to be Prime Minister was to put through a law that people must pass a test for a licence to keep horses. Dora would make up the test.

'Is it all right if I take Hero out tomorrow?' she asked Callie. Hero, like the others, was a Follyfoot horse, belonging to nobody; but Callie had rescued him from the circus, so she was always asked.

'I couldn't even climb into a saddle.' Holding the brush gingerly in her sore hand, Callie was sitting on the back doorstep brushing hay out of her long hair. Whatever she did, even raking a hay field, she always managed to get it all over her hair, face, hands, feet, the pockets of her patchy jeans. 'Where are you going?'

'I thought I'd ride over to the Bunkers' and look at that pony,' said Dora.

'Haven't you got enough horses here to worry about?' Steve called from inside the house.

'Let me go.' She was going anyway, but she wanted to please Steve by asking him. On friendly days like today, when they had all been close and companionable, working together in the hayfield on the side of the hill, with the early summer meadows, patched with buttercups, spreading away to the blue haze of the hills, she wanted to please everybody.

Steve laughed. 'I couldn't stop you. Somebody else's horse is always more fascinating. But for God's sake don't come back with the thing.'

Barney was out in the small paddock at the back of the pre-fab loose box, now smartly creosoted, with a white door and white trim on the window.

'But he's never been in it, the beggar,' Mr Bunker said glumly, 'since Jim turned him out to graze two days after we got him.'

'I can't catch him,' Jim said resignedly.

They stood by the gate, watching the bay pony, head down in the far corner of the paddock.

'You mean, you haven't been able to catch him for two weeks?'

'That's about the size of it,' the father said. 'We tried with oats, we tried with sugar, we tried with carrots. We tried to corner him. We got the neighbours round and attempted to drive him, but he puts his head down and comes at you with his teeth, or else whips round with his heels.'

'What is he like to ride?' Dora asked.

'I don't know,' Jim said. 'I couldn't get the bridle on. That's why I turned him out. But then I couldn't catch him, and I got sick of it. I don't care whether I ride or not anyway.'

'Oh yes you do.' His mother had come out of the house, looking more human in an apron, with a tea towel in her hand.

'He's longing to ride his new pony, but the animal is mad. I rang up Mr Nicholson. "Nothing wrong with it when it left here," he said. "A deal is a deal."'

'I'll bet I know why,' Dora said grimly. 'He knew what the pony was like.'

'Then why did it go so quietly with that girl?'

'Tranquillizers. It was drugged.'

'Oh no.'

'Oh yes. That's what they do. Ron Stryker, a boy who works with us, told me. He's been with second-rate dealers. He knows all the tricks.'

'I'll sue Nicholson,' Mr Bunker said.

'You can't prove anything. The drug has worn off long ago. That's why the pony has gone back to being hard to handle.'

Jim was looking mournful. 'I did like Barney, you know,' he told Dora. 'That first day, when he was nice and quiet, I sat in the manger and told him stories about places we'd go, picnics, and wading the ford, and going up the hill to see the Roman graves. He liked it. He put his ears one back and one forward, listening with one and thinking with the other.'

'Would you like me to try and catch him?'

'Yes, please. Perhaps you can make him quiet again.'

'I can try. He must have been badly treated. Perhaps I can get back his confidence.'

Dora put Hero into the new loose box, where he began to lick the heart out of the bright galvanised manger where Barney had had his last feed. With the Bunkers perched on the gate like crows, she walked into the middle of the paddock and stood still with her hands behind her back. Most horses will eventually come up to you if you stand still. When he came closer, she would breathe at him as if she were another horse, so he could get to know her.

He had his back to her. His head was down to the grass, but he was watching her through his hind legs. She took a few steps forward. Suddenly he whipped round and came at her with his ears back.

Dora was not as brave as all that. She turned and ran.

'Join the club.' Mr Bunker moved along to make room for her on the gate. 'That's what he did with us.'

'What shall we *do*?' his wife wailed. 'We can't just leave him in that field until he dies.'

'You could ring Mr Nicholson and tell him to come and take his pony back.'

'I tried that. "A deal is a deal," he said. He was quite rude.'

'Get me some oats and a rope,' Dora told Jim. 'I'll try again.'

She put the bowl of oats on the ground and stood back. The pony was suspicious at first, but at last he moved forward and began to eat. Every time Dora moved towards him, he flung up his head and backed away. Once he spun round and kicked out.

'Be careful!' the mother called unnecessarily.

The kick had just nicked Dora's hip bone, painfully enough to rouse her fighting spirit. Shutting her ears to Mrs Bunker yelling advice and warnings from the gate, she began to move closer, foot by foot. The pony ate and watched her.

Watching him, she crouched and got her hand on the bowl of oats. He would have stayed while she held it, but Mrs Bunker shouted, 'Hooray!' and Barney jerked up his head and backed away.

Dora turned round angrily. 'You wrecked it.'

'Why don't you go in the house, Marion?' Mr Bunker said mildly, and his wife said huffily, 'All right, I will. I don't want to see her brains kicked out,' as if the whole enterprise were Dora's fault.

Dora started again. At last she was standing with the bowl and the pony was eating from it. She took the weight of it in one hand and inched the other round the rim until she got him! She dropped the bowl and clung on to the halter as the pony pulled her all over the field, dragging her feet through the grass.

'Let go!' Mrs Bunker screamed from an upstairs window.

'Hang on!' Mr Bunker shouted from the gate.

Dora kept talking to the pony, and he was slowing and becoming quieter. At last she managed to get the rope through the halter. She pulled him to a stop and he stood, trembling and blowing. So did Dora. Her legs were like a quivering jelly. But he had given in.

She led him to the gate. The first time she put her hand on his neck, he shied away. The second time, he let it stay there. She told Jim to take out Hero, and led Barney into the loose box, stroking him under the mane and telling him how splendid he was.

'I think he's afraid, not mean,' she told Jim. 'You can tell by the eyes. And the ears. A mean horse will flatten his ears back all the time, but Barney's are—'

Mrs Bunker had come running from the house, crying out how clever Dora was. Outside the stable, she flung up her hand to pat the pony, and he bit off the very tip of her finger and spat it out into the straw.

Dora stayed with Jim while Mr Bunker took his wife to hospital with a bath towel wrapped round her hand. When she came back with the finger bandaged and splinted, they were in the stable and the pony was licking salt out of Jim's hand.

'He's really all right,' Dora said, adding in thought, but not in words, *Unless you go up to him the wrong way.*

'He is not all right. He tried to kill me. We're going to ring the vet and have the pony shot.'

Jim went white. He dropped his hand and ran out of the stable and into the house.

'You can't,' Dora said. 'I mean, it was awful about your finger, and I'm dreadfully sorry, but—'

She looked at Barney, with his honest bay pony head, and felt sorrier for him than for Mrs Bunker. She was in charge of her stupid life. What had happened to him was not his fault. 'Let me work with him.'

'He's got to go.' When Mr Bunker made up his mind, he was unshakable. That was why he was successful in his business. 'I'm phoning the vet. He goes tonight.'

'Then let me take him. Let me try him at the Farm. That family did take Lollipop, so there's room.'

'I don't care what you do with him,' Mr Bunker said, 'as long as he's out of here tonight. Dead or alive.'

Dora snapped the rope onto Barney's halter, mounted Hero, and led the pony down the drive at the side of the quiet old horse.

'Good riddance!' Mrs Bunker called after her hysterically. 'I never did like him anyway. Sir Arthur's boys said he was common.'

# Chapter 10

He was a bit common, with the rather large head and long ears, but not enough to prevent him moving well and freely. He shied at things along the road, and Hero bit him on the neck when he bumped into him. Sometimes he tried to pull away, sometimes he hung back, so that Dora had to drag him along.

It was a very tiring ride. She was glad to see the familiar white gate coming up through the twilight, and the sign: 'Home of Rest for Horses'.

'A home for you, Barnacle,' she told the pony. 'But you're not going to rest too much. You're going to work.'

'What's that then?' Slugger came out of the barn as Dora got off and opened the gate, and walked the horses through.

'I saved the pony's life.'

Slugger sat down on the edge of the water trough and put his head in his hands. 'I give up,' he moaned. 'First that moth-eaten rug on legs, then that nippy Shetland, and now a perfectly fit pony. As soon as the Colonel's back is turned, in they all come.'

Dora did not pay any attention to him. She was walking forward with the horses, watching Steve.

He was standing in the yard with a pitchfork held across his chest like a pikestaff.

'Oh no, you don't,' he said quietly. 'You're not getting away with that.'

'Steve, I had to.'

He was white with rage. His mouth was set. His dark eyes blazed. 'I told you not to bring him back.'

'They were going to have him shot.' It should not need more explanation than that. Steve knew what Follyfoot was for. To save suffering and to save lives.

'We said we wouldn't take in any more horses unless we both agreed.'

'You would have agreed if you'd been there. Those people were raving.'

'You could have come back and asked me.'

'You'd have said *no*.'

'Damn right, I would. I told you.'

'You told me.' Dora's anger was rising to meet his. 'Who says you can tell me what to do?'

Callie came round the corner of the barn, leading two old horses. 'What's that? What a nice pony. What is it, Dora? Can we—? Oh.' She looked from Dora to Steve and back again, feeling the electric rage between them. 'Come on then, Ginger and Prince. This is no place for us.'

Steve did not appear for supper. Conversation was non-existent. Ron was out with a girl. Slugger was sulking. Callie read a school book. Dora couldn't eat.

Dora spent the rest of the evening with Barney, stroking him and talking to him to get him used to his new home. He sniffed at everything – sign of a clever, inquisitive horse. He ate only snatches of his feed, going constantly to the door to look out. When the Weaver banged a hoof on the wall between them, he jumped and kicked out instinctively.

'Are you still in a mood, or can I talk to you?' Callie's face appeared, ready to disappear if Dora growled.

'I don't care.'

'Can I talk to the pony then?'

'Watch out. He's very nervous.'

'What of?'

'I don't know. He's been mistreated by someone. That dealer probably got him cheap.'

'He's nice.' Callie came in and stood by the door with her hands out low, to let Barney get the smell of her.

'If we work with him, he'll be a good ride for you.'

'But Steve says he's got to go.'

'Steve doesn't give the orders here.'

'Someone has to,' Callie said sensibly. 'He's trying to be like the Colonel, you see, saying we can't keep a fit horse when the old wrecks need us. Only the Colonel doesn't get into tempers and charge out of the gate in the truck and nearly kill a woman on a bicycle.'

'Where's he gone?'

'I don't know. He wouldn't speak to me.'

'Nor me either. I hope he hasn't gone to the Bunkers. Callie, we can't let them destroy Barney. Why doesn't Steve see that?'

'He does.' Callie was rather young for her age, but sometimes she was very shrewd. 'But it's got to be his idea.'

Dora could not sleep. She lay awake in the dark, her thoughts going round and round in pointless circles. Very late, she heard the noisy engine of the truck, and the headlights passed across her bedroom wall as Steve turned into the shed.

She heard him bang the door that led to the attic above the tack room where he slept, and heard his feet go up the bare wooden stairs. A horse coughed. Ranger. Another. Lancelot. Wonderboy snorted into the night. She knew the sounds of them all.

Going to the window, she saw the light go on in Steve's room. She wanted to run downstairs and across the yard, and call up the steep stairs to him, 'I'm sorry. Let's be friends again.' Her mind saw her imagined self doing this, but her real self stayed obstinately by the window.

She and Steve did not talk to each other for two days. It was the worst row they had ever had. Worse than the time the donkey scraped him off against a fence post, and Dora laughed at the donkey and Steve thought she was laughing at him. Even worse than the time his beloved old grey Tommy died when he was away, and he said it was Dora's fault.

They communicated through the others.

'Callie, ask Steve where he put the liniment.'

'Slugger, tell Dora I've ordered the linseed and horse nuts.'

Ron Stryker really enjoyed it. He invented messages from both of them, and carried them back and forth to annoy.

'Dora dear, Steve says your stables are a disgrace and you've to do them over.'

'Steve, old fellow, the little lady wants you to come out and see how well she rides the bay pony.'

'Dora, you and his young lordship are wanted in the house. Slugger's made boiled tripe with chocolate sauce and pickles.'

Barney had a lot of fear to overcome and a lot of bad treatment to forget, but Dora worked with him slowly and patiently.

She could see why Jim had not been able to get a bridle on him. First he walked round and round the box so that Dora could not even get the reins round his neck. When she did, he backed into a corner and threw up his head. Being taller than Jim, Dora was able to get her hand between his ears, holding the top of the bridle. Her other hand held the bit against his clenched teeth. She put her thumb into the gap between the front teeth and the tusk and pressed on the gum, but his teeth were still tightly clamped.

'Try sugar.' Callie was watching.

'If I start that, I'll never get the bit in without it. Come in and pinch his nose.'

Several times, Barney managed to jerk his head away, but at last Callie held his nose tight. He snorted, opened his mouth, and the bit went in.

'I'm sorry, Barnacle,' Dora said, as she adjusted the buckles of the bridle. 'But you're too good a pony to be left to rot.'

The first time she got on him, he bucked her off (that was the time Ron called Steve to come and watch).

She got on again, kept his head up, and sent him forward with her legs, and though he jibbed and side-stepped and did not go very straight, he did trot across the field.

Any pressure on the bit made him throw up his head, expecting a jab in the mouth. Winning him back to confidence was going to take time, but he had a comfortable, easy way of going, and Dora thought he had been well schooled once.

# Chapter 11

Steve, who normally would have been as enthusiastic as Dora about retraining the pony, would have no part in it. Even after the row died down and they began to talk to each other again, he still would not listen to her suppertime prattle about the progress of Barnacle Bill.

'You spend too much time with that pony,' he said, 'while we do the work.'

'That's a lie!' Dora pushed back her chair and stood up. 'I do all my work first.' The chair fell into the fireplace.

'Might do that in the winter,' Ron remarked, 'when we're short of firewood.'

'Sit down and finish your supper,' Slugger said.

'I'm not hungry.'

'The pony should be turned out anyway,' Steve grumbled as she went to the door.

'But Dora might not be able to catch him,' Callie said.

As she slammed out of the door, Dora heard Steve say, 'That'll be her bad luck then, won't it?'

The row was still on.

The next day when Dora came back from shopping in the village, she got off her bicycle by the gate at the top of the hill, as she always did, to look out at the stretch of meadows where the Follyfoot horses grazed, or dozed in groups under trees like old men in clubs, stamping the ground bare, flicking idle tails.

The usually peaceful scene was broken up into movement. In the largest field, Barney was chasing round without a halter, nipping and kicking at the other horses.

Dora hurried home, dumped the shopping bags in the kitchen, and tried for more than an hour to catch the bay pony.

The field was too big and the grass was too sweet, and Barney did not want to go back to work. He was not afraid of Dora any more, but he teased her, letting her come near with the rope, even letting her slide the end halfway up his neck, then jerking away and galloping off, bucking and kicking like a prairie horse.

Hopeless. Dora sat down on a tree stump and gloomily tied knots in the rope. After a while, something bumped her hunched shoulders. It was Barney. He kept his head down and let her put the rope round his neck and lead him back to the stable.

Steve was shovelling gravel from the cart into a muddy gateway. Dora had to pass him. She didn't know what to say, so she didn't say anything.

'Took you two hours to catch him.' Steve said it for her. 'Well, he's got to go out, same as the others. No one gets special treatment.'

That was a lie. All the horses got special treatment, according to their needs and natures.

But Dora said, sick of the row, hating the stupid barrier of stubborn pride that had grown up between them, 'I found out how to catch him. Turn my back. Ignore him.'

'You're very good at that, aren't you?'

'What do you mean?'

'Ignoring people.'

He drove his shovel into the gravel and threw it with a rattle and clatter that made Barney jump and pull Dora away.

The row was still on.

It was still stupidly smouldering when Bernard Fox strode into the Farm the next morning, bathed and shaved and laundered and pressed, looking all about him with the bright, critical air of a Lord of creation.

He had come to check on Ron Stryker.

There was a nip in the air today, and Ron had gone back into the tent-like garment which had once been a military greatcoat, years and years ago. The cloth was worn and torn. The ripped pockets flapped like spaniel ears. The buttons were gone and the coat hung open, the trailing bottom edge raking up a line of dust and hay seeds as Ron moved slowly about his work.

From the back, it was hard to see exactly what was moving. Bernard Fox had to ask. Dora looked at Steve, who turned away and whistled. He would not help her out.

'That? Oh – it's Ronald Stryker,' she said. 'The new stable-hand I told you about.'

Ron turned his head at the enchanting sound of his own name. A cigarette hung on his bottom lip. His red hair was held down by a piece of baling twine.

'How do?' He set down what he was carrying and came up with what he fancied was a winning smile. 'Pleased to meet you.'

'And I you,' said Bernard Fox, whose manners were as polished as his boots. 'I'm keeping an eye on things here for the Colonel. He is expecting my advice about employing you permanently.'

'No, he ain't,' said Ron cheerfully. 'Dora's already wrote and got the reply, "Good old Ron Stryker, best news I've heard for months."'

'In those very words?'

'Well, in the Colonel's words. Set him up no end.'

This was a slap in the eye for Bernard Fox, and put him in the mood to find fault with everything.

Ron's coat went first.

'It's nippy today.' He clutched it round him. 'I suffer with me chest.'

'A little hard work will soon warm you up.' Bernard Fox rubbed his hands, and started on Slugger. The old man was scouring out buckets with hot water and soda, wearing an apron made out of a bran sack.

'Looks like hell,' Bernard Fox said. 'What if visitors came in and saw you like that?'

'We run this place for the horses, not the visitors,' Slugger muttered. But Bernard went on, 'Haven't you got overalls?'

There were a couple of brown work coats in the tack room which nobody ever bothered to wear. Slugger was forced into one of them, too big for him, too long in the sleeves. He went on scouring and rinsing, getting himself much wetter than when he was wearing his comfortable sack.

Bernard Fox had the morning to spare, alas, and stayed 'to give a hand'. He found the work of the Farm grossly disorganised, and sketched out a timetable and rota of duties, which he tacked up in the feed shed. He did not exactly hammer in the tacks himself. He supervised Steve hammering.

He supervised the horses coming in from the top field. The Follyfoot way was to open the stable doors, put the feed in the mangers, open the gate of the field and let each horse walk into its own box. They never went wrong. It was a splendid sight to see them come into the yard as a herd, and split up, each with his mind set on his own manger. But Bernard Fox nearly had a fit when he saw this beautiful routine.

'Each horse must be led in and out separately. You can't have them charging about like the Calgary Stampede!'

Anything less like a stampede than the orderly disappearance of hindquarters into doorways would be hard to imagine.

Callie got into trouble for mounting Hero by her patent method of standing astride his neck when his head was down to grass, and sliding down on to his back as he lifted his head. When Bernard Fox objected, she dismounted by her other patent method of sliding down over his tail.

'You are the child who is supposed to be breaking the colt?' Bernard's marmalade moustache was stiff with disapproval.

It stiffened again when he heard about Barney. 'The Colonel has often told me this farm is only for horses in need.'

'He is in need.' Dora's heart sank. Steve was listening. Now he would side with Bernard Fox and Barney would get thrown out. 'He's in need of retraining. Barney's a good pony, but he's been terribly messed up.'

'That's not your job, even if you were qualified.' Bernard Fox did not like to be argued with. 'He should go to a professional.'

'We can't afford it. Anyway, he needs love too.'

'You talk like a stupid girl.'

'I am a stupid girl,' Dora said desperately, hanging on to Barney's halter as if it were her only support.

'And a rude one too,' Bernard Fox said curtly. 'I'd never employ you, and I wonder the Colonel does. Phyllis Weatherby told me a lot of things about you. I've given you every chance, but now I see that it's my duty to write to the Colonel and tell him what's going on.'

'Oh, please—' Dora could hardly speak, but suddenly Steve was there between her and Bernard Fox.

'Don't,' he said. 'Leave her alone. Dora's all right. She's the best worker we've got.'

He was so aggressive that Bernard's boots stepped two paces back. 'We'll see. I'm keeping an eye on all of you, and don't forget it.' He jerked his head at Barney. 'What are you going to do about that pony?'

'Keep it,' Steve said. 'Dora's right. He does need us. There's more than one way of saving a horse. A good one is happier working properly. And Barney will be.'

As soon as Bernard Fox had driven away in his car with the silver thoroughbred on the radiator, they undid all his reforms.

Slugger took off the brown overall and threw it behind the rain barrel. Steve tore down the rota sheet, crumpled it up and threw it at a cat. Callie mounted Hero by sliding down his neck. Ron shrugged himself into his greatcoat again, although the sun was out in warmth. They opened the doors of the horses that had been fed and let them stampede out to graze.

'Yuh-hoo!' Ron gave a cowboy yell as they clattered round the barn and down the grassy track between the fences, stiff old legs stretching gladly, heads forward, snorting, tails up like ancient parodies of colts.

Dora and Steve watched them go.

'Thanks,' Dora said, 'for saving my neck. And Barney's.'

Steve hedged. 'I'm not going to let that Fox come in here and muck us about.'

'But thanks.' They smiled. The row was over.

# Chapter 12

When Dora gained Barney's trust enough to start jumping him, she saw what he really was. He jumped wide and clean, judging his strides to the take off, and cantered on with his eyes and ears on the next jump.

He was a good pony hunter, a bit slow, but a miniature horse without any pony habits. He was still nervous of new fences, but when he knew them, and knew that Dora would not jerk his mouth, he obviously enjoyed jumping. Callie's summer holidays had started at last. She and Dora made a small course of jumps round the outside of the field – gorse stuffed between two fallen logs, sheep hurdles, a couple of old doors for a wall, dead branches piled wide for a spread jump – and schooled him round it with great joy. Not since the days of the grey horse, David, had they had anything so good to ride.

And then of course the Bunkers had to ring up.

They had not bothered to come over and see the pony, but the father rang up after weeks of silence and asked if they had sold Barney for him yet.

'That wasn't the idea.' Dora was taken aback. 'I'm working with him.'

'We're getting another pony for Jim. His riding teacher, Count Podgorsky, tells us we should, and Nicholson says he'll get rid of that brute for me. I want you to take him back there right away.'

'Look, Mr Bunker.' Dora's brain did not always work fast in emergencies, but now it whirled. 'Give me a bit longer.'

'Waste of time.'

'He's shaping into a good pony hunter. You'll get more money for him.' That argument had worked when Dora and Steve wanted to stop the Colonel selling the grey horse, David.

'I'm prepared to take a loss.'

'The Nicholsons took the profit,' Dora said bitterly.

'They've been very decent about it. They're going to find us a top grade pony to make up for our bad luck with this one.'

'Very nice of them.' The sarcasm was lost on Mr Bunker.

'So you'll take him over there?'

'Not just yet.'

'I'll pay you.'

'Oh God, it isn't that!' The stupidity of the whole thing made Dora explode. 'I can't let the Nicholsons sell Barney to somebody else who hasn't a clue.'

'What do you mean, somebody else?'

'Somebody. He's doing so well. Give me a bit longer, please? Come over here, and I'll show you how he—'

'I've no more time to discuss it.' Mr Bunker had exhausted his capacity for talking about horses. 'Sometimes I wish we'd never got into this lark.'

*So do I*, Dora thought, but she said, 'Then you'll leave it to me?'

'Just don't bother me, girl. I'm a busy man.'


Dora and Callie had been riding Barney in one of the old junky saddles. When she heard nothing more from Mr Bunker, Dora went to the local tack shop and bought a second-hand saddle on credit.

'What security?' the saddler asked.

'My wages,' Dora promised. 'I'll pay you something each month.' When she got home with the saddle on her handlebars, she found Ron Stryker fussing with his motorbike. He was wearing his purple jacket with the fringes and his white-trim cowboy boots. They were too tight, so he walked on his heels with the pointed toes turned up.

'What you got there?'

'Grand piano.' Dora lifted the saddle from her bicycle. 'What you got?'

'Three-decker bus.' Ron spat on the rear-view mirror of the motorbike and polished it with his sleeve. 'Want to come?'

'Where are you going?'

'See my mates.'

'What to do?'

'Oh, hang around. Have some laughs. Nothing much. Mystery tour. Come on.'

Dora did not like Ron's mates, but she had nothing to do this afternoon, and she enjoyed riding on the back of the bike with the wind in her face and hair and the speed seeming faster than it was.

Ron wore his flashy helmet with stars and stripes on the front and a skull and crossbones on the back. Dora wore the crash helmet that Callie's father used to wear when he rode Wonderboy in steeplechases, before he died.

The 'mystery tour' turned out to be a horse auction on the outskirts of the town in the valley, a sleazy place of broken-down sheds and cattle pens patched with tin and barbed wire.

'I don't want to stop here.' Dora had heard about these second-rate auction sales to which no one would send a good horse, and no horse lover would send any horse at all.

'Suit yourself,' said Ron. 'I've got a date with one of the boys.' He got off the bike and propped it on the stand, leaving Dora sitting on the pillion in the steeplechase helmet.

Some boys stopped and whistled at her half-heartedly, but in shirt and slacks and the helmet, they were not sure if she was a girl or a boy, so they walked on.

A man in town clothes, who did not look as if he had anything to do with country animals, was leading a skeleton that had once been a horse into a long shed. Dora took off her helmet, shook out her hair, swung her leg off the bike and followed.

Tied along each side of the shed were twenty or thirty of the most miserable horses Dora had ever seen, even in her experience at Follyfoot. Each bony rump had a Lot number on it, like a parcel. There were no partitions between most of the horses. There didn't need to be. None of them had the energy or heart to make trouble.

Dora walked sadly between the skinny hindquarters. The tails seemed to be set unusually low, because the muscle above sloped away.

'Who will buy them?' Ron was down at the end,

talking to a lanky boy with pimples, whom Dora had seen at the Nicholsons' when the Bunkers were buying the pony.

'Dog food makers, some of 'em.'

'I wish we could take them all back to the Farm.'

'Yeah, you would.' Although he pretended to be tough and cynical, Ron had worked long enough at the Farm to have more feeling than he admitted. But not in front of his friend.

'Some of them have been good horses. Look at that head. It could even be a thoroughbred.'

'Oh well,' Ron said, 'we all come to it.' He and his friend from the Nicholsons' turned away, guffawing about something.

Dora stood at the open end of the shed and watched a man in breeches, gaiters and a bowler hat lead a proper horse out of another building where the better stock was. It was a well-bred chestnut, very attractive to look at. It must have had something wrong with it to be sold here, but the crowd gathered round the sale ring as it came in, and the bidding started.

Dora was going out to watch, when she had that feeling that someone was looking at her, concentrating on her from behind, almost like a spoken summons. She turned and saw a rangy cream-coloured horse with an ugly freckled muzzle and enormous knees and hocks, his head turned as far as the rope would allow, looking at her.

'Hullo, friend.' She went back and pushed between him and the next horse to reach his head. It was a big scarred head, fallen in over the pale eyes and nostrils. His tangled white mane flopped on both sides of a heavy neck. The scars on his shoulders showed that he had been driven in a badly-fitting collar.

Dora found crumbs of sugar in her pocket, worse than nothing, because the horse lipped and licked at her hand, desperate for more.

'I would if I could, old friend.' She answered the summons the horse's eyes had sent to her back. 'Mon ami. Amigo. I'd take you home and call you Amigo.'

'You like that old skin?' Ron's lanky pal had come back into the shed. 'One of ours.'

'The Nicholsons'?' She had not seen any horse like this at the dealers' stables.

'He gets bunches in and sells 'em where he can. You can make quite a bit of money, dead or alive. This ugly old hayburner has got a few pulling years left.'

'What will he sell for?'

'About sixty quid. That's the reserve Nicholson puts on all of them. If he can't get it here, he'll get it somewhere else.'

'Oh dear.' In her pocket among the sugar crumbs, Dora did not think she had sixty pence.

'Going to move along then?' Ron's friend watched her suspiciously, as if she might nobble the poor old horse, already nobbled by the years, and working for man.

She patted Amigo on his strong, hard-working shoulder, and went out to the sale ring.

# Chapter 13

There were several young horses up for sale, unbroken, or still very green. One of the best that came out was a strawberry roan, polo pony type, with an exquisite square-nosed head and a straight, springy action. Among the crowd, Dora spotted the Nicholsons: father, mother and Chip, watching it from the rail, sharp eyed.

'New Forest-Arab cross,' the auctioneer described it. 'Rising four, well broke, but green. You'll never see a likelier one, ladies and gentlemen.'

'Likely to go lame,' said a grumbly man next to Dora, who had been crabbing about all the horses.

He was evidently a well-known character here. People laughed, and the auctioneer said, 'I'd back his legs before yours, Fred.'

'Back 'em to kick,' Fred grumbled.

The young roan was very nervous. He threw up his head and stared and snorted. He pulled in circles round the girl who held him. When she lunged him to show how he moved, he put down his head and bucked round the ring, squealing.

'I wouldn't take a chance on him,' the grumbly man said, but the bids were going ahead. You could not always see who made them, because they did not call out. They nodded, or raised a finger without raising their hand from the rail, or coughed, or moved their catalogue slightly. When the roan pony was sold, fairly cheap for what he might become, Dora did not know who had bought him, until she saw Mrs Nicholson lead the pony away, jerking his head down hard when he threw it up in fear of her and the crowd. Dora thought of a slave sold at auction to the highest bidder, powerless over his life, his future unknown.

When she went to get a cup of tea, she found herself standing next to Chip in the line waiting at the greasy snack bar.

'That was a nice pony your parents bought,' she said.

'Mm-hm.' Chip's deadpan gaze considered where she had seen Dora before.

'Is it for you?'

'Till we sell him. I'm going to train him for the race. If he wins, he'll fetch a big price.'

'What race?'

'The Moonlight Steeplechase. At Mr Wheeler's. You know.'

Dora had heard of the Moonlight Pony Steeplechase, which the rich old man at Broadlands organised every year. But it was a posh social affair, with all the 'Best People' in the neighbourhood invited to a champagne buffet before the race, far removed from life at Follyfoot.

But now she found herself envying Chip with the lovely roan pony to train, and the excitement of racing him under the moon over the fences and fields of the pony steeplechase course at Broadlands. And she boasted, 'We may be entering too.'

'You're much too old,' Chip said, as if Dora was fifty.

'We have a rider.'

'What on?' Chip was not really interested, but the snack-bar woman was pouring beer and jokes for a lot of men, and it was a long wait for tea.

'That bay pony, remember, that you sold to those people for their boy. He's jumping like a stag, you wouldn't know him.'

'That thing!' It was the first time Dora had seen Chip smile. She overdid it. She exploded with laughter, slapping her knees, clutching her stomach. 'Well, that's one I won't have to worry about,' she said rudely.

'That's what you think,' Dora said, and when Chip

got her tea first by pushing ahead, Dora jogged her elbow and spilled most of it into the saucer.

It had started as a boasting joke, but the idea took root. Barney in the Moonlight Steeplechase...Dora's mind raced ahead. Callie would have to work hard. They'd make bigger jumps, get him very fit...would Steve and Dora be invited to the buffet supper? She had no proper dress...

She was jogged out of her ambitious dream by the sight of Ron's friend bringing the big cream horse out of the shed and into the sales ring. She pushed through the crowd and stood by the rail, wondering if he would look at her again, trying to send him a thought message as he had done to her: *Good luck, Amigo.*

The auctioneer described him as 'a big strong horse with a lot of work in him yet. Some Clydesdale about him, I'd say.'

'So's your grandmother,' grumbled Fred.

Some man bid a small amount for the awkward-looking horse. He was somewhat over at the knees. He had huge feet like clogs, turned inwards in front and out behind.

'Must be the dog meat blokes.' Ron Stryker had slid between people to stand beside Dora. 'That's about all he's good for, with that leg.'

'What leg?'

'Off fore,' Ron said out of the side of his mouth.

'He's stiff, but he walks sound.'

'Today he does.' Ron winked. 'Nerve block,' he whispered. 'Pheet!' He moved his fingers like pushing in the plunger of a syringe. 'That's why he's stiff. Tomorrow he'll be crippled again.'

The bidding was creeping up. A bent old fellow, in a battered felt hat turned down all round, was raising the bids just slightly ahead of the other man.

'You barmy, Norman?' Fred called across the ring to him.

'He'll pull the log cart.'

Dora remembered seeing the old man once or twice with a thin horse and a big cart piled heavy with firewood. If the cream horse was really dead lame when the injection wore off, and Ron should know after his time with the Nicholsons', Dora had to do something.

Before she knew what she was doing, she had ducked under the rail and run out with her hands up. 'Stop!' she called to the auctioneer, to the old man, to everyone. 'Please stop it. He can't work, he's lame, you can't—'

She was suddenly aware that she was in the middle of the sawdust ring with the old horse and Ron's astonished friend, surrounded by faces and voices.

She swung round. 'Please!' she said desperately. 'Can't you see he's lame?'

Someone laughed. Several people called out. 'What's the matter with her?' the old man complained.

'Go and find out, Norman,' said Fred, and a lot more people laughed.

Dora put her hand on the horse's neck, staring round in fear.

The auctioneer was professionally unruffled. 'The horse is as you see him,' he said smoothly. 'Out of the ring, young lady, and let's get on with it. The reserve is sixty, ladies and gentlemen, or the horse is withdrawn.' He looked at the old man, who shook his head.

'You pig.' It was not said loud enough for the crowd to hear, but Dora heard it, and flinched at the anger in Mr Nicholson's jowly face, scarlet over the rail. 'You pig.'

'Sixty is reserve, I said. If there are no more bids—'

'Sixty pounds.' Dora wanted to speak bravely, but her voice came out in a squeak. 'I bid sixty pounds.'

'And I wish you joy.' Fred's grumble came through the surprised, amused murmur of the crowd.

# Chapter 14

When Dora reached for the halter rope, Ron Stryker's friend said, 'Oh no, you don't. You pay the auctioneer's clerk first. You got the money?'

'Yes,' Dora lied. What on earth was she going to do? She looked for Ron, but he had disappeared. He had probably gone home in disgust.

She went out of the ring to the accompaniment of hoots and whistles and a few corny jokes. In the crowd, a voice said, 'Well done, good girl,' but when she turned – to ask for help, for money, what? – she could not see who had spoken.

She had bought the horse with nothing. What happened now? Would they sue her? Arrest her? The auctioneer's clerk was looking her way, so she turned her back and found herself face to face with Ron, arms folded, head nodding, mouth pursed up tight, appraising her.

'You done it now,' he said.

'Yes.' She could not even make excuses.

'What a spectacle. Christians and lions. Better than *Ben Hur*.'

'Ron, help me. You know these people. What shall I do?'

'Search me.'

'What will happen when they find I can't pay?'

Slowly, very slowly, Ron put his hand into the pocket of his bell-bottom denims. Slowly, very slowly, he pulled out a fistful of something that looked like money. It was money. A tight roll of five-pound notes.

Sometimes Ron had nothing. Sometimes he was loaded. You didn't ask how.

'Ron, you wouldn't—'

Very slowly, licking his finger, he peeled off twelve five-pound notes from the roll. Dora held out her hand. Slowly, licking his finger again, he counted them off into her palm. She closed her fist.

'I can't ever thank you.'

'Shut up.' He would not have it that way. 'It's only a loan, don't forget.'

'I won't.'

'I'll see you don't. You pay me in a month, with interest, or the horse is mine. Agree?'

Dora nodded. There was nothing else to do.

'All of it back in a month, or the horse is mine and I'll sell it cheap to that chap with the log cart.'

The old horse came with her, not willingly or unwillingly. He just came. His enthusiasm for life or any new scene had long ago been extinguished.

As Dora walked away over the trodden grass, she heard a lot of shouting and clatter and saw the Nicholson family shoving the strawberry roan into their trailer by brute force. The ramp banged up and they pulled out of the gate, with the pony neighing and kicking.

Dora and the horse turned into the road and began to plod along. Ron roared past them on the bike as if he did not know them. He had promised to tell Steve to come back with the horse box, but you never knew.

And she did not know if Steve would come.

Dusk came down as she and the horse walked along, and the light slipped away into lilac and green over the line of hills, and stealthily it grew dark.

They were quieter roads now, where the cars did not swish by in an endless stink of noise. Going up hill, Amigo slowed, and she had to walk slower. Would they ever get home? He seemed to be favouring the off foreleg already. If he went really lame, it would take her all night to get back to the Farm. All night and all day. Would Ron tell them where she was? A normal person would, but he might think it a joke not to tell. His sense of humour wasn't normal.

Dora was walking on the right of the road. Lights came towards her and she pushed Amigo over on to the rough grass. The headlights grew, and she saw the small roof lights of the horse box and its familiar bulk, slowing, stopping.

Dora stood blinking in the lights, and leaned against the horse's shoulder, waiting for Steve to get out.

'All right.' He stood behind the light. 'Better make it a good one.'

'The horse is old and lame. Ron thought they'd doctored him to sell. He was being bought to pull a heavy cart. So I – so I bought him.'

'What with?'

'Ron lent me the money. For a month.'

'Then what?' Steve stepped out into the light. He looked at the horse for a long time, and then blew out his cheeks. He and Dora were perhaps the only two people in the world who would not say the cream horse was ugly. He was a horse.

'Which leg?'

'Off fore.'

He stepped round and ran his hand down the canon bone and fetlock. Amigo dropped his head and mumbled at Steve's hair with his loose freckled lip.

'Feels like a splint. And from the scars, that knee could have been broken at some time. But who's going to pay? The Colonel said absolutely no buying. The Farm can't pay for him.'

'I will.'

'How?'

'Somehow. I'll save up my pay.'

'You already owe me most of that on the saddle.'

'I'll sell something.'

'What?'

'Oh – what does it matter?' Dora began to cry. She hid her face in the tangle of white mane that flopped on the wrong side of Amigo's neck, but Steve came round and put his hand behind her head to turn her face towards him. 'What does it matter, Steve?' A cobweb of tears glistened between her face and the lights. 'It's the horse that matters.'

'Dora—' With his back to the lights, she could not see his face. 'What?'

He suddenly put his arms round her and held her very close and tight, so that she had no breath to cry, and did not need to, because she was not afraid any more.

'It's going to be all right. We'll think of something. Come on.' He let her go and took Amigo's rope. 'Let's get this old buzzard home and fed. Get up, horse, you're going to be all right.'

# Chapter 15

The cream horse, Amigo, did go quite lame within a few days, and the vet said there was not much more that could be done. He did not seem to be in pain. They crushed aspirin with his feed to help the stiffness, and turned him out to graze with the more peaceful horses who would not bother a newcomer.

The old horse behaved as if he had not been out to a proper bit of grass for years. When Dora took him to the gate and let him go, he trotted off, dot and carry, his big feet stumbling over tufts. He even tried a canter, pushing his knobbly knees through the tall grass in the corner.

'He looks almost graceful,' Dora said to Slugger, who had come along to help her in case any of the other horses were aggressive.

'Well, almost like a horse, let's put it that way.'

'Look, there he goes.'

Amigo had stopped at a muddy place much favoured for rolling. He pawed for a while, smelled the ground, sagged at all four corners, thought better of it, turned round to face the other way, pawed again, then let himself go, knees buckling with a grunt and a thump as his big bony body went over on its side.

He rolled for five minutes, teetering on his prominent spine with four massive feet in the air when he could not quite roll over. At last he sat up like a dog, lashing the ground with his tail and shaking his head. Prince nipped at him from behind, and he staggered to his feet.

'Poor old Flamingo.' Slugger and Dora turned away.

'His name's Amigo. I told you.'

'That's what I said.'

'No, Amigo. It means friend.'

'Then why don't you call him Old Pal?'


Now Dora had two special projects. Caring for Amigo, and continuing to work with Barney, who was improving every day.

One evening when Callie had jumped the pony well and was pleased with herself and him, Dora confided to her the crazy dream about the Moonlight Steeplechase.

'I'd be terrified.'

'You wouldn't, Callie.'

'The jumps are big and they go flat out for that money prize. Millie Bryant told me. She rode in it last year. She fell off at the water.'

'Barney could do it.'

'He might. I couldn't.'

'You could. I'd ride him myself if it wasn't fourteen and under.'

'Just because you're safely out of it,' Callie said cynically, 'don't pick on me.'

Dora put the idea back into being only a dream. Anyway, Callie was more interested in Folly than in Barney. The colt belonged to her, and she took him everywhere, like a dog, determined that they were going to grow up to have the best horse-human relationship ever achieved.

The relationship was still rather erratic. He would do things for her if he wanted, but if there was an argument, he often won.

'He still thinks he's boss,' Callie said when Folly pulled away again and again to the gate as she was trying to lunge him in a circle. 'How can I explain to him that a horse is supposed to be stupider than a person?'

Sometimes when Dora and Callie were out for a ride with Barney and Hero, they let Folly run with them, if they were not going near a road or sown fields. Hero was his mate, because they shared Callie, and the colt would follow quite well.

They rode one evening down the hill and along a turfy ride at the bottom of a climbing wood. Folly trotting in and out of the trees as if he were a deer. Near the corner, Barney pricked his ears. Dora heard the faint sound of hoofs on the firm, chalky turf.

'Better get off and grab Folly,' she told Callie. 'There's another horse coming.'

Once, the colt had followed two children on ponies home. Once, he had got into the middle of a hunt. Callie did not want to remember that day. The language still burned in her ears.

A boy on a dark-grey pony came trotting round the corner of the wood. Before Callie could get to him, Folly jumped out over the bank. The grey pony shied and the boy fell off.

Dora held Hero while Callie caught Folly and snapped on the leading rein. 'I'm awfully sorry.'

The boy was sitting on the ground, rather dazed, but hanging on to the reins of the grey pony, who stood with its body arched away from Folly, but its neck and head curved round to inspect.

Dora came up. 'Are you all right?'

'I think so.' He took off his riding cap and rubbed his head to see if it hurt. The boy was Jim Bunker.

With the encouragement of Count Podgorsky and Mr Nicholson (naturally), his parents had bought this pony at vast expense so that Jim could ride in the Moonlight Steeplechase.

'Do you want to?'

'No. But my mother wants an invitation to Broadlands.'

Jim was a bit scared of the pony. Her name was Grey Lady, but he called her Maggie, which sounded less scary.

She was a lovely pony, and might give Chip and the roan some hard competition, except for her rider. His lessons with the Count had improved him enormously, but he was still rather sloppy and vague in the saddle, which was why he had fallen off when the pony shied. He had been trotting idly along with a loose rein, admiring the view, quite far from home and totally lost, but expecting eventually to come to a road or a landmark he knew.

After he found out that he had come quite near to the Farm, he often rode the grey mare over to Follyfoot. He would arrive in the morning, trotting on the hard road, or walking through growing wheat, or riding with the girths loose, or doing something else wrong, and liked to stay most of the day, working with the others, or just mooning about. Tennis lessons, swimming, Pony Club rallies, 'meeting nice new friends' – all the things his mother had planned for his holidays – were abandoned, once he discovered Follyfoot.

He had always liked Barney better than Grey Maggie Lady, and he loved the old horses, especially Amigo, who was a dreamer like he was. If the cream horse was lying down in the field, resting his old bones in the sun, he would not bother with the effort to get up when Jim came near. Jim would stretch out behind him with his head against his bulky side, and the two of them would doze off together, under the song of a rising lark.

# Chapter 16

One day when it was too wet to ride, Jim persuaded his mother to drive him over to the Farm. She dropped him at the gate, because she did not want to risk seeing Barney. Even thinking about him made her healed fingertip throb. But when she came back for him that afternoon, Jim was in the barn helping to store bales of hay, so she had to get out of the car and look for him.

She stood in the wide doorway and watched her lanky son heave at the hay with all the strength of his thin arms, which was not as much strength as Callie, even though she was a girl.

'I wish he'd work as hard as that at home,' she told Dora.

'He's good in the stables,' Dora said.

'Not on his own. He has to be driven out to take care of that valuable pony. Boys. Isn't it always the way?'

'Oh, yes.' Dora nodded wisely, as if she had been a mother for years.

Mrs Bunker called Jim to come down from the top of the hay. 'The Drews are coming for dinner. With their daughter.'

'That girl. Why can't I stay here?' Like every other child who became involved with Follyfoot, Jim would rather be here than anywhere.

'Come down, Jimmy,' his mother said mildly, which was how she always talked to him.

'I'll show you all the horses.' He jumped down.

'We haven't the time, and I don't—'

But Jim was already halfway across the yard and waiting for her by the first loose box. He gave her the grand tour, with histories of each horse, which he had learned by listening to Dora and Steve and Callie when they showed visitors round:

'This is the Weaver, who used to be with the Mounted Police until he got the habit of crib-biting. He led all the parades and once he knocked over a man who was going to shoot a politician in Trafalgar Square. This is poor old Flypaper who used to pull a junk cart. This is Hero, rescued from a fate worse than death in a circus ... '

If Slugger was here alone when people came, they got a very skimpy tour, because he would say no more than, 'This here is a old police horse, ruddy nuisance. That's a donkey, been here as long as me – too long. Out in that field, there's a lot of lazy eating machines . . . '

When Jim had dragged her, protesting, round the stables, he insisted on riding Barney in the rain, so that his mother could see how quiet he was now.

Sheltering under a tree with a newspaper over her hairdo, she couldn't believe it. 'Is he drugged again?'

'No, he's himself. I wish I still had him, instead of Maggie.'

'No, you don't, dear. Grey Lady is worth twenty of that common pony.'

'She's got less sense.'

'She'll be the best at the races. Even Sir Arthur's boys with their fancy ponies looked a bit glum when they saw her.'

Dora was in with Amigo when Jim took his mother to see his favourite, bandaging the leg which she was treating with a new liniment.

'What a hideous horse.' Mrs Bunker recoiled as he stretched out his pink freckled nose. Since the accident with Barney, she approached a horse very cautiously, with her hands in her pockets, which meant sugar to Amigo.

'Ssh. He's got troubles enough without hearing that.'
Jim knew about Dora's money problems. Everyone knew.
Ron Stryker teased her about it all the time, counting up
the days until he would, as he said, 'foreclose the
mortgage'.

Kneeling in the straw, tying the tape of the bandage,
Dora had one of her wild, impossible ideas.

There seemed to be plenty of money for buying ponies,
loose boxes, recently a trailer for Grey Lady, an Italian
saddle, expensive breeches and boots for Jim. The Bunkers
had taken up horsiness in quite a big way. Mrs Bunker
wore a Pony Club badge on one lapel, and on the other a
glittery horseshoe brooch. Could Dora ever find the nerve
or the words to ask her for a loan of sixty pounds?

While she was searching for them among the jumble
of ideas and impulses and half-formed sentences
scrambled in her head, Jim told her, dreaming with his
shoulder against Amigo's wide chest, 'If Maggie and I win
the steeplechase, we'll give you the prize money for
Amigo.'

The prize money was a hundred pounds. Colossal
largesse from colossally rich Mr Wheeler, who did not
think in figures of less than two noughts.

Dora sat back on her heels. 'You wouldn't.'

'Why not? We wouldn't want the money, would we,
Mum?'

'For you to win that race will be reward enough for me.'

'I don't much want to ride in it, you know,' Jim said.

'Of course you do,' his mother said firmly. 'It's the chance of a lifetime.'

For her to get into Society at Broadlands. As the parents of a competitor, she and her husband were sure of an invitation to the champagne supper. As mother of the winner, she would be the equal of anybody. If Jim and Grey Lady were first past the post, it would be the crowning triumph of her life.

Grey Lady had a chance. She was a marvellously built pony, very fast and a bold jumper, though she made mistakes sometimes with Jim because he was nervous.

Now that Amigo's future hung on the race, Steve began to train the grey mare when Jim brought her over to Follyfoot. They had built some larger jumps and a longer course. It included jumping the stone wall onto the lawn, over the rose arbour which had fallen in the last storm, and out again by way of the trench they had dug from the drainspout so that rain and sinkwater would keep it wet and boggy. This was good practice for the notorious Broadlands Water jump, uneasily nicknamed Beecher's Brook.

Steve was in his glory with such a good pony to ride. Jim let him do the training. He would rather ride Barney, or potter about on the donkey, or sit high on the ridge of Amigo's back as he ambled about the field.

Dora too preferred to ride Barney. Although she wanted Grey Lady to win the money for Amigo, she still wanted Barney to be in the race, for his experience and her pride.

'You still think I'm going to ride him?' Callie asked, after the ponies had completed the course, with Dora a hundred yards behind by the time she lurched over the drainwater jump and into the last stretch over the hurdles to finish at the dead tree in the orchard.

'I know he hasn't a chance, but still.'

'If he hasn't a chance,' Callie said, 'I don't mind so much.'

'What do you mean?' Dora slid off the sweating bay pony.

'It was the idea of having to try and win I couldn't face. You know I hate contests.' Callie suffered tortures in exams or on School Sports Day, or at the kind of parties where they played competitive games. 'But if it's just for fun, then I wouldn't mind so much.'

That evening, they sat at the kitchen table to make out the entry for the Moonlight Pony Steeplechase.

'Give us a bit of paper,' Ron said. 'I'm entering me old pal Amigo.'

'He's not yours.'

'He's as good as mine.' Ron never lost an opportunity to make a joke about the loan that was not really a joke.

'If you're riding that Flamingo,' Slugger saw Dora's face and tried to make it into a real joke, 'I'm entering the mule.'

'Too old,' Callie said without looking up from what she was writing.

'What do you mean, too old?'

'He must be nearly twenty.'

'Oh.' Slugger sat back. 'I thought you meant me.'

On a clean sheet of paper, Callie, whose handwriting was the best, copied out the entry:

'Barnacle Bill. Bay gelding. 14.1 hh. 7 years (he was nine, but seven looked better). Rider: Cathleen Sheppard. 12 years. Colours: blue with gold cross.' (Her father's racing silks, much too big, but Dora would take in the seams).

Callie read it out.

'Disqualified already.' Ron was picking his teeth with a chicken bone. 'Warned off the course.'

Callie and Dora stared at him.

'Barnacle still belongs to the Bunkers. Ponies must be ridden by their owner. Chip told me when I was down at their place last week to see how she's going with that roan.'

'How is she going?'

'Lovely.' Ron made a circle of his thumb and forefinger, and kissed it into the vague direction of the Nicholsons' stable. 'Makes Grey Maggie whatsername look like a plough horse.'

'We'll see,' Steve said.

'But if I'm not going to win,' Callie was working carefully on the flourishes of her signature under the entry form, 'cheating won't matter. It's just for fun, isn't it, Dora?'

'Yes.' But secretly, crazily, Dora had never stopped dreaming that the bay pony might win the race. 'Just for fun.'

# Chapter 17

Barnacle Bill was too slow. Dora gave him plenty of oats and plenty of galloping, and also walked him endlessly uphill to develop his muscles, but he was not built for speed, and he did not have the speed.

Dora thought he was galloping faster, until she went with Steve and Ron to a meeting at the racecourse near Bernard Fox's stables and saw the thoroughbreds run. That was really galloping.

It was a flat racing course, a mile oval of beautiful turf, with the double line of rails newly painted, and the red-brick stands and buildings bright with white paint and window boxes. There were flowers everywhere, and neatly-trimmed evergreens. Even the bookies, on a lawn by the grandstand, looked more colourful than usual, with bright umbrellas up not for the rain, but the sun in a dazzling sky.

Ron Stryker went to every race meeting and came back a plutocrat or a pauper, usually a pauper. Steve and Dora did not go often, because they had no money to lose, and if you followed Ron's tips, you lost, even when he mysteriously won. But on a fine day this course was attractive and the races were exciting, and it was easy to see all the way round without buying a grandstand ticket.

Dora stood by the rail of the paddock all the time the horses were being led round before the race. She could never get enough of watching that marvellous swinging thoroughbred walk, the arch of the fine-skinned neck as the horse caught impatiently at the snaffle, the muscles moving under the shining skin, the whole bloom of a perfectly fit horse from the tip of the slender curved ears to the brushed tail swinging like a bell. Dora envied the stable lads and girls who led the horses, but they looked quite unexcited. So did the owners and trainers as they chatted in a sophisticated way in the centre of the paddock. Only the jockeys, when they came out, gave a hint in the eyes and mouth of being tense and excited, although some of them who had been riding for years joked casually, as if riding a race at thirty miles an hour were no more than going to the cinema.

When the horses went out to canter down to the start, Dora pushed through the crowd to get a place on the slope of grass at the side of the stands. From here you could see the whole race streaming round the course like a train; turning the bend, and head on into the straight, pounding, thudding, the leading jockey glancing back, each horse's head going like a piston, its hoofs reaching for the turf and flinging it behind, a galloping marvel.

They were made for speed, and made for a course like this where they could gallop flat out. The pony course at Follyfoot was full of odd quirks and corners, rough ruts and soft patches, muddy wallows through gateways, short stretches of grass where you could let your pony go if you were sure of stopping him in time for the bend round the tree and the tricky hop onto the bank, with a drop into the lane. If Barney could only gallop here, he might learn to stretch and reach and gallop out, as the thoroughbreds did.

Dora was standing among the cheering and clapping people round the unsaddling enclosure, watching the pretty woman owner in a white dress and sandals who was holding her horse's bridle, when the idea came to her.

'Good race, Jessica!' someone called, and the owner waved to them in the crowd. She patted her horse's dark soaked neck and smiled for a man with a camera, wrinkling her eyes against the sun.

When the Pony Steeplechase was run and won, it would be moonlight, not sunlight, in which the winner would stand, with the cheers of praise all round.

Mr Wheeler always picked a date when the moon would be full. If it was cloudy, the race was put off to a clear night. The course was lit by the moon, with flood-lights in the trees at the start and finish, and the headlamps of cars positioned to light jumps without dazzling.

This was the great risk and venture of the race, which some people (not invited to the supper) said would need to have a huge prize to get anyone to enter. No one, they grumbled, but an old fool like Mr Wheeler, who had been a daredevil rider in his day and was said to have broken every bone in his body, would dream up a night-time race. Although horses, like many animals, can see better than people in the dark, ponies who galloped and jumped well out hunting or in training would be much more uncertain and nervous under the moon.

But if Barney could gallop here on the racecourse, if he could learn to gallop by moonlight, flat out with confidence on the smooth turf...

# Chapter 18

Dora did not tell anyone her plan. She could not even tell Callie, because if she knew how serious Dora was about training Barney, she might refuse to ride in the race.

'Just for fun,' she had insisted. But there was nothing funny about sneaking Barney out of the small field at night, and riding him down the moonlit lanes into the valley and up the other side to the racecourse.

This was serious. Dora had turned him out tonight, so that Steve would not hear him come out of his box and across the cobbles. She had taken his saddle and bridle from the tack room where Steve slept above, and hidden it in the woodshed. She had gone upstairs with Slugger and Callie, and then dropped silently from her window into the tomato bed, using a branch of lilac to swing herself down.

Barney was easy to catch these days, as long as you pretended you did not want him. If you stood still in the field, not looking at him, he would come up and drop his mealy nose into your hand and practically beg you to take hold of the halter.

The moon was three-quarters full, bright and pearly. A fairly strong breeze blew small clouds across it, but they were gone quickly. Barney trotted quite happily in the half dark, his big ears alert to the unfamiliar black and white landscape, but without shying or stumbling. Dora would be able to let him gallop flat out. Neither of them would be afraid.

The main entrance to the racecourse would be shut and locked, but Dora knew that she could go round to the far side, where there was a gate used by the man who grazed a couple of horses on the grass in the middle of the course. They lifted their heads as Barney came in, and one of them called, but as he trotted down the side of the course to the stands, they dropped their heads again, well used to seeing horses gallop here.

Dora went through a gap in the rail, dismounted, and took Barney into the paddock. Walking casually with a blade of grass in her mouth like one of the stable girls, she led him round, and imagined that thoroughbreds walked in front and behind her, and that the knowledgeable crowd were standing round with astute comments, and people like Ron were giving people like Steve unreliable tips about what and what not to back.

Her other self was there too, at the rail, watching herself with envy.

She was also there in the middle of the paddock as an owner, chatting easily with the woman in the white dress, and with her trainer, who bore a resemblance to Bernard Fox, except that he was polite to Dora, and with her jockey, who nodded briefly as she wished him 'good luck.'

Then she was the jockey, coming out a bit-bowlegged. She mounted, touched her cap to her invisible self as owner, nodded at a last minute instruction from Bernard Fox, rode out and cantered down to the start.

Barney trampled as she collected him, and closed her legs against his sides.

They're off! He bounded ahead, and settled down to drum the turf in a steady gallop that seemed, that was, faster than he had gone before.

He galloped so fast that the wind roared in Dora's ears as if she were flying in an open plane. He galloped halfway round the course before he slowed to a canter, and finished with his head down, blowing, the streaks of foam on his dark wet neck white in the moonlight.

The crowd went delirious. They cheered and shouted in the stands. They threw caps in the air, and crowded round Dora as she came off the course, reaching out to touch Barney.

Well done! Good race! The winner, the winner!

Dora got off Barney, and invisible hands slapped her on the back. She led him into the small unsaddling enclosure with the little room where the jockeys weighed in after a race.

She stood there with Barney, his neck steaming under her hand, his nose squared, in and out, to get his breath back, and peopled the rail with admiring faces, and imagined the applause and the excited voices and the click of cameras.

'Oh, my God. Oh, good God, I can't believe it. I absolutely and finally will not believe it.'

The vision fled. The cheers of the crowd faded. Dora and Barney stood alone in the empty unsaddling enclosure. Behind them at the gate were three men. One was Bernard Fox.

'Get that animal out of there.'

Dora led Barney out, feeling more foolish than ever in her life, which had already included many foolish moments.

'I dread the answer,' Bernard Fox said, 'but I'll have to ask you to explain.'

'I didn't think anyone would be here.'

'We happened to have a late committee meeting, and that's a better explanation than yours. A thief climbs a drainpipe and gets in through a bedroom window. He's at the jewellery box when the woman pops up in bed. "A burglar!"'

Bernie was showing off for the other men.

'The thief shoots her dead and takes the diamonds. When they catch him, he explains, "I didn't think anyone would be there."'

The other men, one tall, one small, laughed. Dora did not crack a smile. Barney put his head down and cropped the short clovery turf.

'You'll have to think up a better excuse than that, Dorothy.'

'You know the girl?' The tall man looked at Dora down his long nose.

'She works for the Colonel at Follyfoot Farm. Mad as hatters, the whole lot of them. And the Colonel's the maddest to leave them on their own. I'll have to write to him again,' he told Dora, 'so let's hear your reason for trespassing.'

Dora shook her head, 'There isn't any.'

She could not say, 'I'm training the pony for the race.' They would say, 'What race?' and laugh when they heard. She thought of the marvellous big horses streaming round at thirty miles an hour. They would laugh at poor little

Barney with his burst of speed that ended in a canter.

'I can't make sense of it,' the small man said.

'These young people,' the tall man said, 'they just want to barge into other people's property as an act of rebellion.' He put on the voice with which grown-ups who can't remember what it was like to be young tell each other what the young are like.

'A revolutionary, eh?' The small man was quite twinkly and nice.

'Nothing so dashing.' Bernard Fox would not let it improve to a joke. 'She's a trespasser, and should be prosecuted. I shall write to the Colonel and warn him, in case the committee decide to tell the police.'

'Please don't.'

He did not answer, so Dora got on Barney and walked away. Before she turned out of sight behind a clipped hedge, Bernard Fox delivered his parting shot.

'And you're too big for that pony.'

# Chapter 19

As the night of the race approached, excitement grew. Stories kept coming in about the other competitors, mostly exaggerated for good or bad.

Mrs Bunker reported that Mr Bunker had been up at the squash court at the Manor and had seen one of Sir Arthur's ponies jump almost five feet. The carpenter had measured it.

Jim reported some highfaluting claims that Count Podgorsky had made about one of his other pupils.

But Jim had also seen the pupil fall off. 'For no reason. She rides worse than me, if you can imagine that.'

Steve had heard from the feed merchant that Mrs Hatch from the Pony Club was buying cough medicine for her daughter's pony.

Ron was still hanging about with his pal at the dealers, keeping out of sight of the Nicholsons, but watching the roan pony, now fancifully named Strawberry Sunday.

'That's your competition,' he told Jim. 'The Nicholsons have made up what they like to call their minds that they're going to win. When they go after something, that lot, they get it. It's not only the money and the sale of the pony, see. But people round here don't think so much of them. They gotta win, see, and show who's best.'

'That's that, then.' Jim was sickeningly defeatist. 'If they're the best, they'll win.'

'You've got to win.' Steve made a fist and held it under Jim's pointed chin. 'Think of Amigo. Get out of here, Ron. You're bad news.'

'I'm only saying what I see. Just thought you'd like to know, that's all. I seen that strawberry roan last Saturday gallop alongside their big thoroughbred, and she was right there with him all the way.'

Steve groaned.

'Just thought you'd like to know.' Ron went across the yard, chucking a pebble at a swallow swooping under the barn roof, and out to his motorbike.

'I thought you were going to help me hang that gate,' Dora called. 'Where are you going?'

'Down the Nicholsons'. I got everybody here all

sweated up about the roan. May as well get Chip into a lather by telling her how good our grey is.'

The excitement began to build up in the neighbourhood. Among people involved with the race, who talked of little else, it became clear that Strawberry Sunday and Grey Lady would be the favourites.

Poor Barnacle Bill. If he could not even gallop a mile on the flat, he would be lucky if he finished the steeplechase course at Broadlands. He needed to work, so Dora went on training him and Callie, if only to keep herself from worrying about what Bernard Fox and the committee were going to do to her.

*What had he written to the Colonel? What would the Colonel write to Dora?* She still had not told anyone about the moonlight gallop. One morning she almost told Steve, but when she opened her mouth the words sounded foolish before she even got them out.

'Steve.'

'What?'

'Nothing.'

'Get a move on then. Maggie's all tacked up. I'm going to race you and Barney across the big stubble field.'

'Let Callie ride him.'

'Why not you?'

'I think I'm too big for him.'

'Since when?'

'I just think so.'

Why care what Bernard Fox had said? But when someone you don't like tells you something you don't want to hear, you do care. You even begin to believe it.

After Steve and Callie had ridden off, Dora heard his bossy voice.

'Anyone about?' He was calling out of his car window, as if he expected a reception committee.

Dora ducked into the tack room. She heard the car door slam and his boots in the yard. No escape. Bernard would be sure to snoop in here to see if they had cleaned the tack, so she nipped up the stairs and hid in Steve's room.

Crouching by the window, she heard him talking to Slugger.

'Where is everyone? The place is deserted.'

'No, it ain't. I'm here.'

'Where are those lazy kids at this time in the morning, with all the work to be done? Look at the bedding. Hasn't been mucked out for days by the look of it.'

'Well, you see, it's like this.' Dora heard Slugger go into the slow, maundering voice he put on to annoy people who annoyed him. 'That there is the Weaver's stable, that is.'

'It's a dirty stable. I don't care whose it is.'

'Ah, but if you knew the Weaver. Very messy, he is. I knew a horse like him once, long ago, before the war it must have been. Big brown horse with sickle hocks. Name of... name of, what was that beggar's name?'

'Where's Dorothy?' Bernard interrupted.

'In the tack room,' Slugger said. 'Cleaning tack.'

'I'm glad to hear it.' Dora heard him open the door and shut it. 'If she was, she isn't now, and from the look of the tack she ought to be. I can't stop any longer. I came to tell her I'd heard from the Colonel.'

'Oh yes?' Slugger was interested. Dora's heart fell into her stomach like a stone.

'He said he'd written to the Farm and settled the matter. I wanted to know what he wrote.'

The stone leaped out of Dora's stomach, suffocatingly into her throat.

The Colonel had settled it. How? The sack? When the letter came, she would not be able to read it.

But after she heard Bernard's car leave, and turned to go down, she saw the letter with the familiar writing and the foreign stamp on Steve's table, she had to pick it up. It was addressed to Steve, but she had to read it.

*Dear Steve,*

*I owe you a letter, so I'll send this one to you.*

Sitting on the unmade bed, Dora glanced through the first pages, which were about the villa and his health and some people they had met who used to breed hunters, and some details about the Follyfoot horses, and the forms from the Ministry of Agriculture.

On the next page, her name stood out from the Colonel's scrawly handwriting as if it were up in neon lights.

'*So Dora has been having some fun. Never a dull moment, eh? I've calmed Bernard Fox down, but tell her to watch her step like a good girl. We don't want any trouble at the Farm. The old horses come first.*'

When Steve and Callie came back, with Barney very blown, Grey Lady still on her toes, Dora said, before Steve had even got off, 'I read the Colonel's letter.'

'In my room?'

'I was making your bed.' It was still unmade. 'No, I wasn't. I was hiding from Bernie.'

'Oh God, is he—?'

'It's all right. He's gone. He wanted to find out what the Colonel wrote. So did I. So I looked.'

'You read other people's letters.'

'You don't give other people's messages. Why didn't you tell me what the Colonel said?'

He turned away from her to dismount. With his face to the pony, putting up the stirrup, loosening the girth, he said, 'I didn't want you to know I knew.'

'But you don't know what I did.'

'No, but I thought if you wanted me to know, you'd tell me.'

He did not ask a question with his face or voice, so Dora said nothing.

He led Grey Lady away. Dora went back to work.

Steve was the best friend Dora had ever had. He had told her once that she was the only real friend he had ever had. But sometimes they could not talk to each other.

# Chapter 20

Three days before the race Mrs Bunker came over to Follyfoot, white and shaken.

She had been woken in the night by the barking of her miniature poodle, who wore a jewelled collar and slept on her bed.

'Mimsy was quite hysterical. I knew she'd heard something. So I put the sheet over my head and sent Mr Bunker down to investigate. He took his gun. I told him not to, because it's worse to kill someone than to be burgled, but he took his gun and when I heard the shot, I thought my heart had stopped.'

She put her hand on her heart, to make sure that it was working now.

Mr Bunker had seen a figure in the shadows by the

gate of Grey Lady's paddock. As he came closer, the gate swung open. He shouted, and the figure – man? boy? girl? He couldn't see – ran off. He fired a shot after it.

The shot had woken all the neighbours and, as Mrs Bunker had predicted, caused more trouble than the intruder. Mr Bunker was to pay a fine for possession of a shotgun without a licence, and Mrs Bunker had been embarrassed by stares in the supermarket, because word had spread round like a bush fire that he had shot her.

Worst of all was the knowledge that someone was trying to sabotage Grey Lady.

'I think they were either going to kidnap her, or turn her loose to get killed on the road.' Mrs Bunker's eyes were round with horror. 'Who would do such a dreadful thing?'

Ron snickered. 'I got a good idea.'

'The Nicholsons?' Dora said. 'Oh, that's absurd.'

'I told you they were desperate to win the race.'

'And you've been scaring them about Grey Lady.'

Ron laughed. 'Shook 'em up a bit, didn't it?'

'Better put a padlock on the gate,' Dora told Mrs Bunker.

'I told Jim to keep the pony in the stable,' Steve said.

'She bangs her foot on the door in the middle of the night,' said Mrs Bunker.

'Hang a sack full of gorse on the door,' Steve said, 'and put a dirty great padlock on the bolt.'

'And on your oat bin,' Ron added darkly. 'There's some people will stop at nothing.'

How much did he know? The curious thing about Ron was that he could seem to be on everybody's side at once. He was mixed up in all sorts of things without ever actually taking part or getting caught. He lived on the fringes of many worlds – the Farm, the racecourse, horse trading, the motorcycle gangs – without belonging completely to any of them.

It was even impossible to find out whose side he was on to win the race – Strawberry Sunday or Grey Lady. He was taking bets on it, illegally. Ron would take or make a bet on anything. How many palings in a fence, or red cars passing in the next mile, or grains of maize in a handful. What time the rain would stop. What tin of soup Slugger would open for lunch. 'Two to one against tomato. What'll you bet me?'

Dora found him looking thoughtfully over Amigo's door as the raw-boned old horse dozed in a shaft of sunlight, resting one back leg, his hip bone sticking up like the peak of Everest.

'What will really happen if Grey Lady doesn't win the money and I can't pay you back?' she asked.

'I told you. The old skin will be mine.'

'You don't want him.'

'He'd fetch a bit. The firewood chap still hasn't got no horse for next winter.'

'You wouldn't really—'

'You think I'm soft, don't you, girl?' Ron made his tough face, jaw twisted, eyes narrowed, talking what he thought was gangster American out of the side of his mouth. 'You might get surprised one of these days.'

Ron was away from home that evening, 'checking on a few situations.' He never said exactly where he was going, or who he was going to see.

Before they went to bed, Steve and Dora decided to go and look at a situation of their own.

'I'm still worried about Maggie,' Steve told Slugger. 'We're going down to check the padlocks and make sure everything's all right.'

'And get a load of bird shot where it hurts,' Slugger said. He began to push aside the clutter of mugs, letters, ornaments, combs, books, pebbles and hair clips on the wide shelf above the fireplace.

'What are you doing?' Callie asked.

'They'll be needing to eat breakfast off the mantel-piece tomorrow.'

Dora and Steve left the truck down the road from the Bunkers' house, and walked barefoot up the drive. All was dark and quiet. No lights in the house. Padlocks on the loose-box door and on the oat bin in the shed.

Grey Lady had been lying down, but she got up nervously, and watched them over the door as they padded about, looking in sheds and behind bushes, up into the trees and down into the non-existent depths of the ornamental well.

Often they stopped and listened to the normal noises of a suburban night. Two dogs barking back and forth. A rooster who had set his alarm clock too early. A radio. The throb of drums from some distant café, the beat without the music. The endless faint roar of cars on the main road beyond the hill whose edge was rimmed with brightness from the stream of lights.

Nothing to see. Nothing to hear. Dora stopped again. Something to smell? She raised her face like a dog and put her hand on Steve's arm.

'I smell smoke.' She gripped him tightly.

'A chimney?'

'No, nearer.'

They were by the bottom fence, looking for the footprints of the intruder at whom Mr Bunker had fired. As they ran back to the stable, the smell of smoke grew definite, grew stronger.

Steve shone the torch round the outside of the loose box. The grey pony was banging against the gorse-filled sack on the door. Dora pushed her head aside and saw, at the edge of the straw, a billow of smoke that burst, even as she looked, into a crackle of fire.

Uselessly she pulled at the padlock, bruising her fingers and yelling for Steve.

'Get her out! We've got to get her out!'

As smoke began to fill the stable, Grey Lady plunged against the door, wild-eyed. Steve wrenched at the padlock, and swore.

'Get up to the house,' he told Dora. 'Wake them. Get the key.'

Dora ran. She beat on the door of the Bunkers' house and shouted. It seemed an eternity before a window went up and a head in a hair net looked out.

'Go away. You're drunk.'

'The stable's on fire!' Dora was gasping for breath, her throat full of smoke fumes. 'Get the firemen. Give me the key!'

'Oh, my God.' The head went inside and shouted, 'James, James! Where's the key?'

'Key, what key?' A sleepy rumble.

'Grey Lady's stable is on fire. Oh, my God. Oh, my heart.'

'Hurry!' Dora yelled. The fire would take hold fast

in the straw bedding. She might already be too late to save the pony.

When the key came sailing out of the window, she scrabbled for it in a flowerbed and ran, choking with fear and the acrid fumes ahead. Gasping and sobbing, she turned the corner of the stable and saw Steve raise a huge stone in both hands and crash it down on to the bolt. Something snapped. The door splintered open, tearing away at the hinges, and fell with a noise like a cannon as the pony trampled over it and off into the night.

Running behind her, Steve and Dora heard the tattoo of her hooves on the road. They followed as far as they could in the dark, but she had run on the hard road and left no traces. They did not know where she might have turned.

'Let's go back and ring the police. Someone will stop her.'

A fire engine was in the drive, pumping water into the stable. The Bunkers stood desolately in their night clothes. The father chain-smoked nervously. The mother in her hair net clutched her shivering poodle. Jim was crying.

He ran to Dora. 'Where's Maggie?'

'She ran off but she'll be all right. We'll find her.' She put her arms round him. His thin body was trembling, even though it was a warm night.

Neighbours had come from all round. Raincoats over pyjamas. Mothers carrying babies. Barking dogs. Old men coughing. Children frantic with excitement. It was not until the fire was almost out, and smouldering sullenly in the wreck of the stable, that Steve and Dora saw that one of the people in the watching crowd was Ron Stryker.

'What on earth?' Steve grabbed him from behind and spun him round.

'Hands off. I didn't start it.'

'Who said you had?'

Ron always made excuses before he was accused.

'The fire engine passed me on the road. When I saw where it went, you could have knocked me down with a—'

'How did you know who lived here?'

'I didn't. I saw poor old Jim. What are you two doing here for that matter?'

'We came to check. We were here when the fire started.'

'Oh yeah?' Ron leered.

*What did he know? Was he mixed up in this himself?*

Dora pulled Steve back into the shadows. 'He couldn't possibly—?'

'He may know who did.'

'If anyone did. It could have been an accident.'

One of the firemen, who had been looking for clues, came out of the loose box with something in his closed hand.

'People who smoke in a stable,' he said, 'shouldn't be allowed to keep horses.'

'I'm always careful.' Mr Bunker ground out a cigarette under his foot, but almost at once his hand went to his pyjama pocket and he lit another.

'But you were out here late this evening, you said.'

'To make sure the pony was all right before I went to bed.'

'Excuse me.' The fireman went up to him. 'Is that a filter?'

Mr Bunker took the cigarette out of his mouth and showed him the filter tip.

'Thank you.' The fireman opened his hand and showed what he had found in the straw. The white plastic filter of a cigarette.

'It couldn't have been me.'

His wife and son were looking at him. Jim was still crying. Mr Bunker was blustery and red, as if he would cry too. 'I told you. I'm always careful.'

'Someone wasn't,' the fireman said.

Dora looked at Ron Stryker. Under the lank red hair, his face showed no expression. If he did know anything, he would never tell.

Accident or arson? To Steve and Dora it did not matter. All that mattered now was finding the terrified grey pony.

# Chapter 21

In the morning, the police had heard nothing. Dora and Steve spent all day until dark driving round asking people, following up false leads, getting nowhere. Grey Lady had vanished.

'She'll never come back.' Jim was heartbroken. The pony meant much more to him now that this terrible thing had happened.

'I'll get you another,' his mother said automatically, but she was desolate too, her dreams of the race and the party and the glory all shattered.

'I'll never ride again,' Jim said, with a long white face of tragedy.

His mother was too upset to tell him, 'Yes, you will.'

*

The next day, the day before the race, Dora rode Barney out alone all morning, following the way Jim used to ride between his house and Follyfoot, turning into farms where the grey pony might have gone looking for other horses, searching woods and thickets where she might have run blindly in and got caught up in the undergrowth.

'How do you expect that poor little beggar to run tomorrow?' Ron asked when she brought Barney back at midday, tired and sweating.

'We're not going to the race.'

'Don't be daft. I may get my money from you yet. He and Callie will have a better chance.'

'Not against the roan. They've got what they wanted.'

'You're not thinking—?' Ron looked shocked.

'I'm not thinking anything,' Dora said wearily. 'I don't know what I think any more. Come on, Barnacle, if you've finished your lunch, we're going out again.'

'Take it easy,' Ron said cheerfully.

Steve was out with the truck, looking hopelessly round the roads, while Dora rode hopelessly on the field paths. They met in the lane that ran along the bottom of the gorse common. Dora came down the bank with Barney, and found Steve sitting on the bonnet of the truck eating a sandwich and staring moodily across the broad valley. Cows and sheep and distant horses grazed, and tractors moved across ridged fields, you could not have recognised a grey pony even if it was somewhere there.

'Any clues?'

'Only negative. I've just rung the Bunkers,' Steve said. 'The police still haven't heard anything.'

'It's hopeless, isn't it, Steve?' Dora got off Barney and let him tear grass off the bank.

'Not yet. If she'd been hit on the road, the police would know.'

'Suppose we never hear anything?'

'Then we'll never know. It will be like that poor dog Roger, who went away when he was ill.'

'I hate that. It's better to see an animal dead than not know.'

'No.' Steve shook his head. 'It's better to go on hoping.'

'I wish you had the horse box instead of the truck,' Dora said. 'Poor old Barney could get a lift home.'

'He's all right. He's so fit. It's a shame he can't do the steeplechase course.'

'I couldn't go, could you, Steve?'

'Not without Maggie. Not without at least knowing where she is.'

It was quite a long way home. Dora pushed on, trying to keep out of her mind the terrible visions of the beautiful grey pony smashing into a speeding car, lying out somewhere with a broken leg, stolen, abused perhaps, chased by shouting boys with stones, running into wire in her panic.

Barney was fit enough to trot steadily along, but at a crossroads where they should have gone straight on, he stopped and tried to turn left, and would not answer the pressure of Dora's legs.

'Come on.' He was never like this now. He had become a calm, trusting pony who never shied or stopped or whipped round.

He stood like a mule, listening with his big ears.

'All right.' Dora heard hooves too. 'So there's another horse somewhere. There are about ten thousand horses in this county. If you stop for every one of them, we'll never get home.'

It was a grey pony. It moved from the shelter of some overhanging trees. Barney called. The pony lifted its head and broke into a trot, its rider wobbling bareback, hanging on to a halter rope with one hand and the mane with the other, red hair flopping.

'Told you to take it easy, didn't I?' Ron grinned. 'Whoa, Maggie.' He hauled the pony in and slid off, wincing. 'I'm as sore as the old lady who rode the cow.'

'How on earth did you find her?' Dora could speak at last.

'How on earth?' Ron mimicked her. 'Not, "Thanks,

Ron dear," or, "Oh you clever boy." Just, "How on earth did *you*, a dope like you—?"'

'Oh, shut up.' Dora was so relieved that laughter came easily. Or was it tears that wanted to come? 'Oh Ron, I don't care. I'm just so glad she's all right. You don't have to tell me anything if you don't want to.'

'Like what? You accusing me of something?' Ron's eyes were sharp. 'Just because I've got a lot of good friends who keep their eyes peeled and their ears to the ground – contortionists, they are – and know everything that goes on, I'm always getting accused. Going to have it on my tombstone. "Ronald Arbuthnot Stryker. Always Accused."'

'Where was she?'

'Man found her over Harlow way. Run herself into the ground, she had, and he got a halter on her. Seeing she was classy-looking, he was going to keep her in hopes of a reward. I persuaded him different.'

'How?'

'I have my methods.' He closed one eye. With Ron, you never knew whether to believe the whole story, or part of it, or none of it.

Dora asked him no more, and he told her no more.

# Chapter 22

Steve was wild with joy. Everybody was. Apart from a few nicks and scratches on Grey Lady's legs, and a piece of skin torn off her shoulder, she had not suffered from her terrifying adventure.

The run across country and the long jog back with Ron had calmed her down. The Weaver was turned out, and she walked peacefully into his loose box and put her pretty head straight into the manger to lip up the chaff the finicky old horse had left.

'She'll be all right to race tomorrow.' Steve brought her a big feed. 'Ring up the Bunkers, Dora, and tell them she's here. They'll hit the ceiling.'

Dora was heading for the house, but Ron stopped her.

'Are you mad? After all I've been through to get that

animal back. There's still tonight, you know. There's still *danger*.' A word Ron loved.

'He's right,' Steve said. 'Let's keep her hidden.' He came out of the loose box and shut and bolted the top door. 'Don't trust a soul.'

'I must tell Jim, and put him out of his misery. He can keep a secret.'

'It wouldn't need words to give it away. He's got to keep his misery, right up to the last moment when we tell him he can put on his new boots and his mum can put on her new dress and meet us at Broadlands. And then watch some people's teeth gnashing!' Steve gnashed his own like castanets.

'You still don't think it was Mr Bunker's cigarette?'

'I'm not taking any chances. I'm going to see that pony win tomorrow if it's the last thing I do.'

Dora went to tell Amigo. 'All is not lost, old friend.'

He had never thought it would be. He hung his heavy head over Dora's shoulder and dreamed of an eternity of easy living.

'Even if Grey Lady doesn't win,' she told him. 'I'll get your money somehow.'

She heard Steve call Callie to go and clean Barney's saddle and bridle. There was that too. The saddler was getting a bit restless. She ought to be worrying, but somehow, standing in the stable with her kind old horse, sharing his content, it was hard to worry.

No time for worrying the next day. No time for anything except finishing the work of the Farm and then starting to get Grey Lady and Barnacle Bill ready for the Moonlight Steeplechase.

'Since it's going to be run in the middle of the night,' Slugger grumbled, 'it hardly seems worth using all my washing-up liquid on the manes and tails. "Makes your dishes sparkle like the dewy morn."' He picked up the empty bottle and read the label. 'Fat lot of good it's going to do Maggie and old Barn to be sparkling like the dew when there's thirty ponies kicking mud in their faces, all shoving together at Beecher's Brook with the banks like a sponge.'

'They won't get mud in their faces,' Dora was plaiting Barney's wet mane, and spoke through a mouthful of rubber bands, 'because they'll be in front.'

'I don't like it.' Slugger shook his head and stuck out his lower lip. He had never liked it. 'If the Colonel was here, he'd not let you go.'

'If the Colonel was here,' Callie said from underneath Barney, where she was trimming his heels with Anna's scissors, 'he'd be at the front of the crowd yelling, "Legs, dammit, legs! Where's your impulsion?"' Memories of her jumping lessons with the Colonel.

'It's all right for them that can watch the race.' Slugger sniffed. 'But how'd you like to be left here biting your nails and wondering who's coming home on a stretcher – you or that pony?'

'Oh, *thank you* for minding,' Callie said.

But Dora, realising what was behind the grumbles, said, 'Of course you're coming, Slugger. You've got to come.'

'Didn't get no invitation, did I?'

With Callie's parents away, Dora and Steve had been sent their invitations to the supper party.

'You're the groom,' Dora said. 'We've got to have a groom. All the posh people will.'

'What about me?' Ron asked. 'If it wasn't for me, there wouldn't be no Grey Lady.'

'So you'll be her groom. Two ponies, two grooms. I told you we were going posh. You can wear Steve's jodhpurs.'

'Like hell he can,' Steve objected. 'What'll I wear?'

'You'll wear the suit.' Steve had only one set of garments that could reasonably be called a suit.

'Only if you wear the dress.' Dora had only one dress that could reasonably be called suitable for Mr Wheeler's party.

Two hours before it was to start, Dora rang up Mrs Bunker. 'Yes?' Jim's mother had been answering the telephone with this dead voice ever since the disaster of the fire, expecting no good news.

'Put on the red dress, Cinderella. You're going to the ball.'

'What ball? Don't play tricks with me, Dora, I've got a splitting head.'

'Take an aspirin. You're going to Mr Wheeler's champagne supper.'

'It's only for people who have a child in the race.'

'But you have! You have! Grey Lady is here and we're taking her over to Broadlands with Barney. I can't explain now.' Dora cut short a babble of excitement from the other end of the wire. 'Just get yourself and Jim dressed, and we'll see you there.'

'He's gone to bed. He's exhausted.'

'Wake him up. Give him some vitamin pills. Tell him he's going to win!'

# Chapter 23

Steve's jodphurs were too big for Ron, who was less muscular. He reefed them in round his waist with his gaudiest tie, and put on his pointed cowboy boots and a sinister long black sweater. He added an Indian headband and a tin Peace symbol – Peace, for someone like Ron who was always making trouble! – on a thong round his neck.

Slugger looked less sensational, but more correct. He had brushed and pressed his Army breeches, and Dora had sewn a leather patch on the frayed elbow of his tweed jacket, and found him a check cap of the Colonel's. They stuffed it with newspaper to keep it off his ears.

Callie, with her hair in two tight pigtails, wore her father's blue and gold racing silks proudly. Steve borrowed

Ron's orange shirt to go with the suit. Only Dora was still in her old bleached jeans as they loaded the ponies, rushing Grey Lady into the box as if there were spies everywhere.

Dora had the yellow dress and sandals in a paper bag under the front seat where the five of them sat crushed together, singing 'One Meat Ball' to keep their nerves calm. The moon was up and full, its mysterious face half smiling in a cloudless sky.

'I wish it was raining.' Callie shivered.

'Nervous?'

'No. Yes. No.' Callie looked at Steve. He was nervous about Grey Lady. He did not want her to be nervous about Barney. 'I'm excited, that's all.'

'He'll go well for you.' Dora squeezed with the arm that was round Callie to make more room. 'He's a good pony. The best.'

'If everybody else dropped down dead,' Ron said. 'The waiter *roared* across the *hall*, "We don't serve bread with one meat baw-haw-haw!..."'

At Broadlands, Dora changed into her dress in the horse box, combed her hair and put on the sandals. Barney was being walked round by Slugger, bow-legged, very horsy, eyeing the other ponies under the peak of the Colonel's cap. Grey Lady was still in the horse box. They would not take her out until just before the race.

On the terrace in front of the big pillared house, the local socials were drinking and chattering. Coloured lamps hung in the white portico and along the windows of the great house. There were candles in glass bowls on the little supper tables. Yellow flares streamed dramatically from the balustrade.

Floodlights in the trees lit the wide sweep of parkland that was the start of the course, and its finish. Beyond, at the bottom of the slight slope, you could see the first fence, a brush jump, clear and black in the moonlight, and beyond that the post and rails, and then the corner of the copse, where they would turn across a stony road and over the bank. Headlights of cars, parked to light the tricky take-off, silhouetted the young trees.

Dora had walked the course twice with Callie. She knew every jump, every turn and stretch of rough going. It looked very different now, the fences bigger, the rails more solid, the grass waiting white and challenging for the charge of galloping hoofs.

Steve and Dora managed to get themselves on to the terrace by climbing over a dark corner of the balustrade, to avoid coming up the main steps in the light and the stares. They stood shyly in a corner, and a waitress brought them something on a silver tray which she said was ginger ale, but which tasted in Dora's excitement as if it might be champagne.

They saw Sir Arthur and his wife, very much at ease, talking about 'the tribe', as they called their three sons, who were indistinguishable in looks and behaviour, except that the youngest was even ruder than the others.

They saw the local Master of Foxhounds, a television personality who would rather be behind his pack than in front of the cameras. They saw Mrs Hatch of the Pony Club, with her picket-fence teeth, and the famous horse-master Count Podgorsky, slim and elegant, with shining hair and shoes apparently made from the same material.

They saw the Nicholsons, beefy and too loud in this company, talking up 'fantastic' horses they had for sale, and putting down a great deal of champagne with their little fingers crooked, to show they knew what was what.

They saw – help! – Bernard Fox's crinkly ginger hair moving through the gathering towards their corner, an amused smile lifting his marmalade moustache.

'Dorothy?'

'Hullo.' The yellow dress had felt all right, but instantly it felt all wrong, and Dora knew it was too short.

'I hardly recognised you. You look very nice.'

'Thanks.' Dora tried to move behind a small table, because he was looking at her legs.

Bernard Fox stayed, smiling at her, twirling his glass. He was obviously trying to find some slightly less insulting way of asking, *How on earth did you two get here?*, so to get rid of him, Dora said, 'We brought the bay pony. The Colonel's stepdaughter is riding him.'

'Done any training gallops lately?' Burnished Bernie was mellower tonight. It must be the champagne.

'Oh yes.' Dora glanced at Steve. She still had not told him about the racecourse, in case he thought it was silly. 'At the Farm.'

'Good girl.' Bernie laughed at her, and then wagged his head and chuckled to himself, 'Couldn't believe my eyes,' remembering Dora in the unsaddling enclosure.

'What did he mean?' Steve whispered when he finally moved off.

'He couldn't believe seeing us here,' Dora said.

'I didn't like the way he looked at you.'

'Nor did I.' But Dora took a quick look down at her brown legs, and could not help feeling a bit pleased that Bernard Fox had admired them.

The Bunkers had still not arrived.

Suppose they never came. Suppose Jim refused to ride. Suppose Mrs Bunker refused to come to the party because it was too late to go to the hairdresser. Suppose Mr Bunker had put his foot down because he was still upset about being suspected of causing the fire.

Steve and Dora went through a dozen anxieties. Below the terrace, the young riders were having a picnic supper on the grass, their coloured shirts and jerseys vivid in the light of the flares. They looked over the edge and saw Callie eating stolidly. Saw several girls in a group, giggling. Saw others sitting alone, too nervous to eat. Sir Arthur's boys throwing food about. A tall boy in glasses who looked too old to ride. Mrs Hatch's daughter with her teeth spaced like her mother's. No Jim.

'If they don't show up, I'm leaving,' Steve fretted. 'Ron can drive the box home. I'll hitchhike.'

'May as well have the supper,' Dora persuaded him. But although the guests had begun to help themselves from the long buffet tables at the back of the terrace, piled with marvellous-looking food, she and Steve were too shy to push through the chattering crowd, who juggled plates and forks and glasses, looking for places at the table.

'Come on, come on, you've got no supper.'

A short old man, twisted like a dune tree, limped up to them, leaning on a knobbly stick. He had thick white hair, eyebrows like fluffs of cotton wool, and a pointed white beard. His face was aged and lined, with faded-blue eyes that smiled at them, a more simple, direct face than many of the others here.

'It's – you're Mr Wheeler, aren't you?' Dora asked, embarrassed because they had been too shy to speak to him when they arrived.

'Forgive me for not greeting you before,' he said, removing her embarrassment. 'You're from Follyfoot

Farm, aren't you? Steve and Dora. Good. Good.' He had a way of looking at you closely, not staring insolently like Bernard Fox, but attentively, as if it mattered to him to know what you were like. 'Come on. Get some food before the savages devour it all.'

He went with them to the buffet, and even asked the butler, who looked more like a bishop, to take special care of them.

The butler carved beef paper-thin and delicate rolls of ham, and helped them to pile their plates with chicken, salad, pastry shells filled with creamy shrimp, something in aspic, pickles, olives. He invited them to come back for more, and when he had turned away to open bottles, Steve managed to sneak a plate of food and two glasses of champagne out to the far corner of the terrace, so that Slugger and Ron could reach up for them later.

# Chapter 24

After the ice cream and little coloured cakes, Mr Wheeler stood at the top step of the portico, leaning on his stick, and made a short speech about the Moonlight Steeplechase.

'I stole the idea,' he said, 'from those famous Cavalry officers of some hundred and fifty years ago, who were sitting round after dinner one night, drinking brandy and wondering what kind of lunacy they could think up to pass the time.

'They all had good horses in the stables, and as the moon was bright, they set out to race each other across country for the tall church steeple which stood up miles away in the moonlight. Using a steeple for a landmark gave us the name Steeplechase, as you know.'

He beamed down on his audience, who nodded and murmured, whether they knew or not, to show that they did. The Master of Foxhounds said, 'Jolly good luck to 'em,' and Mr Nicholson belched a champagne bubble and said, 'Hear, hear.'

'With white nightshirts over their Mess uniforms, and white nightcaps over the brandy fumes in their heads, they rode straight and reckless, taking everything in their path, over, under or through. Tonight, we have the more civilised course over my land, but the young riders will take it just as hard and straight and courageously as those first Midnight Steeplechasers.'

'For a hundred pounds, who wouldn't?' muttered Mrs Nicholson, the same shape all the way down from her square shoulders to her hips in a dress like a sack. She looked at Steve and Dora. 'I know you, don't I?' and turned away, not caring whether she did or not.

Mr Wheeler was announcing that since the young riders were the most important guests tonight, he would introduce them all to the rest of 'this brilliant company'.

He called out the names, and they stood up in their colours, Callie blushing furiously, caught with a piece of cake in her mouth. 'Cathleen Sheppard on Barnacle Bill.'

Dora cheered, and Mrs Nicholson turned round and gave her a look.

'Betty Hatch riding My Pal' – applause. 'John Deacon,' the tall boy with the glasses ('How old is he?' from Mrs Nicholson), 'riding Challenger' – applause. 'Linda Murphy with Lassie' – applause, loud from her own family. 'Chip Nicholson riding Strawberry Sunday' – applause, and a whistle from her father, made socially bold by champagne.

Chip stood up unsmiling, disowning him, chunky and workmanlike in good boots and white breeches and a red and white striped racing shirt.

'John So-and-so on Geronimo. Joan This-and-that on Black Velvet... Jim Bunker... Where are you, Jim?'

A slight figure idled across the grass, pale-faced under the flares, swishing a thistle with his whip, flop of hair over his narrow forehead.

'Just in time. Good boy. Jim Bunker, everybody, just in time.'

'My mother got her zip fastener stuck,' Jim said unconcernedly.

Laughter.

Poor Mrs Bunker, arriving so flustered and late in her red dress with the sequin top, the laughter met her as she came up the steps, Mr Bunker close behind, as if to stop her from turning tail and running.

But Mr Wheeler, who was terribly nice to everybody, came down from the portico and greeted them warmly, and took them to get food and wine. She must have broken the zip. The back of her dress was sewn up with big stitches, perhaps by her husband. Poor Mrs Bunker. Her night of glory.

But there was still Grey Lady.

All the ponies were to parade in a circle of turf marked off below the terrace. Steve got the grey pony out of the horse box, while Slugger put Dora's saddle on Barney.

Jim ran up, carrying his saddle, dropped it on the ground, and flung his arms round Maggie's neck.

'Don't make a fuss,' Steve told him. 'We don't want the Nicholsons to know she's here till the last minute.'

He saddled her up behind the box, while Slugger took Barney and walked round with the other grooms and stable girls and big sisters and mothers of the riders. Barney looked his best: mane neatly plaited, tail plaited at the top because there had been no time to pull it; heels and head and ears trimmed; white star and hind socks washed and rubbed with chalk, gleaming in the moonlight. Slugger plodded with his head down, because that was the way he always walked, but he wore a grin of pride.

Callie stood in the middle with the other riders, riding cap jammed down tight, biting her lip, arms folded over the blue and gold silks.

'I wish the Colonel could see them.' Dora nudged Steve.

You could tell which family owned which pony, they each watched their own. Only the Nicholsons were shrewdly assessing the field.

There were twenty-eight of them. The roan had not come in yet, and Ron had been told to bring Grey Lady in last. He passed behind Steve and Dora with his mouth full and a glass in his hand.

'Where's Maggie?'

'Tied to the back of the box for a moment while I got the supper you left me.' He wiped a hand across his lips. 'Ta.'

'Bring her in now.'

Strawberry Sunday had joined the parade, with Ron's lanky friend leading her. Then Ron brought in Grey Lady, on her toes, jogging, reaching at the bit like a little race horse.

Dora and Steve watched the Nicholsons. If they were shocked, they did not show it. They stared at the grey as they stared at the other ponies, with a dealer's eye, shrewd, calculating, not giving away admiration or contempt.

The television MFH, who was in charge of the race, gave the order to mount. The riders joined their ponies among the trees at the edge of the floodlit strip of grass that swept down to the first jump.

Dora, more nervous than Callie, gave her last minute instructions to which she did not listen. 'Don't push him at the start. Take the bank turn wide, give him room to stand back. Remember there's a ditch on the other side of the cut-and-laid. Watch that little chestnut – he kicks.'

Chip was up on the roan, point-to-point saddle, stirrups very short, rubber racing reins.

'Is that the same bay pony?' Under the pulled-down peak of her cap, her face was deadpan, like her parents. The jeer was in her voice.

'Looks a lot better, doesn't he?' Callie said, naïve and friendly, but Chip had moved on.

Dora saw Jim go over to Grey Lady among the people and ponies by the trees. There was a flurry of excitement. Someone shouted. She ran, and pushed through the crowd. Grey Lady's saddle had slipped round, and Jim was lying on the ground, whimpering and holding his wrist.

'Who did up the girth?'

'Don't look at me.' Ron, with his headband and his Peace symbol, was holding the nervous grey pony.

'I did. I know it was tight.' Steve was kneeling by the boy on the ground, but was pushed aside by a sobbing woman in a spangly red dress who flung herself on her son.

'My boy, my boy! I knew something like this would happen.'

Although the whole thing had been her idea: buying the pony, teaching Jim to ride, entering the Steeplechase.

'It's all right, Mum.' Jim stopped whimpering and sat up.

'He put out his hand as he fell,' Steve said. 'The wrist is either broken or badly sprained. There's a doctor here. Someone's gone to fetch him.'

'It's all your fault,' Mrs Bunker said hysterically, on her knees in the tight dress, trying to get her arms round Jim, who was trying to keep her away from his hurt wrist. 'Who asked you to bring the pony here?'

This was so fantastically unfair that Steve did not answer. He got up, took Grey Lady from Ron, and went with Dora out of the crowd, as the doctor came to Jim.

'I know that girth was tight, Dora.'

'Ron left Maggie to get his supper.'

'And his pal was late bringing the roan in.'

'Because he was loosening the girth?'

'By God,' Steve said bitterly. 'By God, I hate to see them get away with it. This pony could have won.'

He hunched his shoulders, looped Maggie's reins over his arm, and slouched towards the horse box, swinging Jim's riding cap by the elastic.

News of the accident had spread among the riders, who were collecting for the start. Callie trotted back, her eyes dark with anxiety in a white face.

'They said it's Jim.'

Dora nodded. 'He's all right. But he can't ride the pony.'

'Oh, poor Maggie.' Callie thought of horses first. 'Poor Jim – oh, Dora, the prize money – poor *Amigo*!'

'Listen, Callie.' It all came into Dora's head at once, just as if it was written down in a book and she was reading it. 'Grey Lady can win. You ride her, Jim can pretend he's given her to you before they take him to hospital. Mr Wheeler won't mind, because of the accident.'

'But you wanted me so much to ride Barney.'

'That doesn't matter now. Winning matters.'

'I can't. Maggie's too fast. I can't ride to win.'

'You can. You must. Think of Amigo, Callie, we can't let the Nicholsons get away with this.'

'They did it?'

'I think so. Are you going to let them win?'

'Steve!' Callie shouted, her voice shrill with excitement. 'Bring Maggie back!'

# Chapter 25

'A bad start,' the television personality called out in his voice that was familiar in the homes of almost everyone there. 'But it's going to be a good race. The moon is up. The ponies are fit. The riders are shaken, but not unstrung.' Only one girl, who was a mass of nerves anyway, had got off after what happened to Jim, and refused to get back on. 'Five minutes, everybody, to get settled down again. Five minutes till line up.'

Callie was on Grey Lady. 'Jog her round,' Steve said. 'Get the feel of her.'

'I know her.' Callie gathered up her reins, confident now and not afraid. 'Sorry, Barnacle. He would have liked to run, Dora.'

'He's going to.' Once more the book of ideas was open

in her mind. 'Hold him a minute, Steve.'

She ran to the horse box, pulled on her jeans, stuffed the short yellow dress into them, kicked off her sandals and trod into her old shoes. Steve was still holding Jim's riding cap. Dora grabbed it and shoved it on her small head, tipping it down over her face.

'Who's that child in the yellow shirt?' someone asked as she joined the others, letting down her stirrups as she went. Dora did not hear the answer. But they thought she was a child. All right, Barney. You shall have your race.

The television star was holding up a flag, while he tried to get the twenty-nine ponies into some sort of line.

'Back the brown pony, bring up the little chestnut, come on, that boy in the green shirt. Look out, no barging. Yellow girl on the bay, get on the end there. All right, all right, everybody—'

At the end of the line of stamping, jostling ponies, Barney was wildly excited. His days of lawlessness came back to him. He trampled, grabbing at the bit. Dora shortened her reins. He reared up slightly, pulling, and just when she thought she could not hold him, the flag came down and he plunged forward in the galloping surge of ponies.

Whatever instructions had been given to anybody not to go flat out at the start of the race were forgotten, or impossible to obey. Big ones, small ones, Welsh, New

Forest, cobby ones, they all went full tilt down the floodlit stretch of the park, and by some miracle were over the strong brush jump and pounding towards the post and rails.

Someone refused and swerved into someone else, who swore like a grown-up – Sir Arthur's youngest. Dora had to pull Barney sideways. He got too close to the rails and had to cat jump, landing short and losing ground. Dora gathered him together and he settled down to gallop his own steady pace in the middle of the field. Grey Lady and Strawberry Sunday had pulled out ahead. Some of the smaller ponies were already falling behind.

Wide at the turn into the bank, Dora had told Callie, and she told it to herself now as they came to the corner of the copse where the lights of the parked cars illuminated the grey and the roan with haloes for a moment as they reached the top of the bank together, and dropped down with a switch of their tails.

To get up the steep bank, you had to take off from the stony road, not put in a stride on the grass. Dora swung into the light, saw people standing by the cars, a man on the roof with a film camera – one stride into the road, and then she gave Barney a kick that propelled him from his strong quarters to the top of the wide bank. He changed legs and jumped out into the drop, wide and safe.

Beside him, a pony stumbled and fell. Its rider pitched forward, and one of the people scrambled up the bank with a shout. Don't look back. Never mind the others. It was a dangerous race, but even if they all fell, Dora and Barney must keep going, their own line and their own pace. That was how she had planned it with Callie.

As each jump came up – the cut-and-laid, the narrow brush, the hedge with the guard rail, the little ditch – Dora only had time to see that Callie was over, and then it was she and Barney. He took off too soon at the cut-and-laid, dropping a leg in the ditch. He was bumped at the brush, stirrups clashing, by the tall boy, who turned his head and shouted at Dora, although it was his fault, glasses spattered with mud. He stood back beautifully from the guard rail, clearing the hedge by miles. He tried to stop at the dry ditch, because the moonlight looked like water in it, which he hated, but Dora forced him over by strength of will as well as legs, and he jumped straight into the air, much too high, and landed stiff-legged, with Dora hanging on to his mane, because she knew he would jump it like that.

Several ponies seemed to have dropped out, or else they were far behind. Dora was in a middle bunch, Grey Lady and the roan and about half a dozen others were ahead. Jumping well, Barney gained ground at the fences, but lost it in the fields between. But the pace was fast, and the others were slowing too. Dora passed the Hatch girl, floundering across a ridge and furrow, and someone else on a long-tailed black, who ran out at the low wall. Barney was still going steadily, but he was tired. Anything might happen at Beecher's Brook.

It was the last fence but two of the Steeplechase course. It came after the final turn towards the home stretch, a stream with sticky banks, which ran across a corner of the park, in view of the spectators at the top of the slope.

After the brook, there was a hurdle jump, then a low rail between two trees, nothing much. But Broadlands' Beecher's Brook had floored many ponies who were galloping home to win, and Dora, as she cantered across stubble, hopped a double rail into the park and saw the water gleaming, thought that it would floor her too.

Callie and Chip were still yards ahead of anyone else. Grey Lady did not mind water, and if the roan jumped badly here, as most ponies would, Callie could pull ahead and Chip might not catch her.

Headlights of cars gilded the surface of the running brook. Grey Lady went fast at it, and almost stumbled in the soft footing. Callie checked her for the take off, and she was in the air when the roan came sideways into her and they fell together on the other side, floundering in the marshy ground.

Dora saw Grey Lady struggle up. She must get to Callie. Barney stopped in a bunch of ponies, trampling the sticky ground suspiciously. Barney, you must! Dora held tight for the enormous jump that he would make over the hated water, and almost fell off when he suddenly dropped his head, and charged through the water into the mud on the other side. The dreaded brook was only a few inches deep here, and he was clever enough to know it.

And there was Callie standing up, hatless, filthy, waving to show she was all right, waving Dora on, as the other ponies splashed and floundered over the brook behind her.

Someone was alongside her at the hurdles, and hit them with a rattle. She was alone over the low rail. Barney pecked, recovered, and plodded into the floodlights, to pass the white post at the top of the slope in barely a canter between the cheering, whistling crowd.

Barney stopped of his own accord. A riderless pony crashed into him, and the rest of them pulled up in a tangle.

Slugger was running bandy-legged, his mouth open in a shout. 'Barney!' Crumpled newspaper flew out as he tore off his cap to wave it.

'Dora!' Steve jumped down from the balustrade of the terrace, and as Dora dropped off Barney, he flung his arms round her in a hug that nearly broke her ribs.

'You won.' He held her off and grinned at her before he turned and ran down the slope to Callie.

# Chapter 26

A lot of people were running. Callie was walking forward with Grey Lady. Chip was sitting on the muddy bank, and Strawberry Sunday stood with her head low, one foreleg dangling.

'My God, it's broken!' someone called, and Dora saw the Nicholsons' lanky boy, Ron's friend, throw down a cigarette and run towards the brook.

She left Barney in the crowd and broke away from the congratulations and the flashbulbs, and walked to where he had dropped the cigarette. It was still smouldering. Dora trod it out, then bent and picked it up, looked at the white filter, and put it in her pocket.

'Who is it? Who won?'

Mr Wheeler, field glasses round his neck, limped

down from the terrace steps.

'Run down to the brook,' he told a boy, 'and tell me what's happened there.'

The crowd separated. As Mr Wheeler reached out to shake her hand, Dora took off her cap and shook out her short hair.

'Dora?'

'I'm sorry,' she said. 'I'm too old to be in the race, but I didn't mean to win.'

'It was a great race anyway,' Mr Wheeler began, but parents and riders were clamouring at him with protest and argument.

'She's too old.'

'She's disqualified.'

'My boy was second.'

'No, I was.'

'Tortoiseshell was second.'

'Without a rider, stupid.'

'Mr Wheeler, Mr Wheeler, it isn't fair—'

'Quiet, everybody!' he bellowed with surprising volume for so old and small a man. 'Dora won, but she can't win. We know that. So whoever came second—'

'I did.'

'It was me.'

'My daughter was well ahead.'

'I saw it, I tell you, it was Bazooka.'

'I was in front of him.'

'I was.'

'Bazooka…me…my daughter…' But since the race had no second prize as nobody had really seen, in the excitement, who was next in the bunch behind Dora and the loose pony.

Mr Wheeler took her arm and walked with her and Barney under the trees, away from the lights and the squabble.

'I can't give you the money,' the old man told her, leaning on her arm, 'so I'm going to give it where it's needed. I'm going to give it to Follyfoot. You won it, you can spend it how you like. For the old horses.'

The boy he had sent down to the brook panted back.

'The roan pony pulled a tendon. Not a break, but it's pretty bad. The Nicholsons are wild. They say the grey jumped across her.'

'*She* knocked into the Grey Lady!' Dora was furious. 'I saw it. It was delib—'

'I saw it too.' Mr Wheeler cut her short. 'But let it go. The pony's badly hurt.' He sighed. 'A sad ending to something that perhaps I never should have started. I'm not going to run any more Steeplechases, Dora. Not at night. Not for money, anyway. Money spoils everything, doesn't it?'

Dora didn't know. She never had any.

*

When Dora gave Ron back his sixty pounds for Amigo, he pulled a bulging wallet out of the inside of his jacket and added the money to a considerable wad of notes.

'Ta,' he said. 'And for the rest of it. Always a picnic for the bookie, when an outsider wins.'

'But the race was a washout,' Steve objected. 'Those people may want their money back.'

'They can sue me then,' Ron said smugly, 'and admit they placed illegal bets.'

'Money spoils everything.' Dora echoed Mr Wheeler.

'Speak for yourself.' Ron put the wallet back inside his jacket and swaggered off.

By the time Jim's broken wrist was healed, and the plaster cast had been taken off, Grey Lady had been sold to a hunting family who would use her well. Jim was to have Barney back.

'But don't worry,' he told Dora. 'I'll ride him over to the Farm mostly, and he can see all his friends. I'd let you keep him, but Steve says he knows you can't keep a fit pony here.'

'*I* know we can't,' Dora said. 'Steve's not the boss. We both are. We both know what Follyfoot is for.'

It was very sad when Mr Bunker rebuilt his stable, and came for Barney with the trailer behind the red minibus.

Dora watched it pull through the gate, and went out into the road to see the last of Barney: rounded bay quarters, black tail hanging over the ramp, the net up front swinging as he pulled contentedly at the hay with a horse's trusting ignorance of parting.

The trailer disappeared round a corner. Dora went back into the yard and got a wheelbarrow and fork and joined the others at work.

As she backed out of Amigo's stable, a man's voice behind her said, 'Excuse me, miss.'

Dora set down the barrow.

'I've got my cattle truck outside,' the man said. 'I found this wretched horse. Belonged to a neighbour of mine, who went away for a bit. I thought he'd told somebody to look out for the horse, but when I went by his place, I saw he'd simply left him. In a little yard. No grass. No more hay. Water all gone.'

'How *can* people—' Dora started out with him towards the truck.

'They do.' The man shook his head. 'I've been abroad. Egypt, South America, India. I've seen how they treat horses. But this poor fellow...I can't take him, so I thought of you. When I couldn't get an answer on the phone, I pushed him into the truck and brought him over. I know there is always room here for a horse in trouble.'

'Yes.'

Dora called Steve, and they went out to the horse. He was so starved and weak, they could hardly get him out of the cattle truck. He walked with them slowly on his shaky legs into the loose box that used to be Barney's.

'Here!' Slugger was filling a bucket at the tap. 'I just cleaned that stable out.'

He brought the water over, and they watched the horse suck it in through his wrinkled lips, and then he sighed, holding the last of it in his mouth, and dribbled it slowly over Dora's hand.

'One day,' Slugger picked up the bucket and turned to fetch more water, 'one day we'll keep an empty loose box here. That'll be the day.'

# Follyfoot

## MONICA DICKENS

Follyfoot farm is a home for rescued and unwanted horses, and the animals are cared for by the stable-hands Callie, Dora and Steve. There's plenty of work to be done around the farm, but there's still always time for the mysteries and adventures that happen at Follyfoot.

Visitors are welcome at the farm, but when two boys come snooping round and obviously aren't interested in the horses, Callie is suspicious. She's sure she recognises one of them. But where from? The mystery deepens and it's up to the young stable-hands to get to the bottom of it.

The long-awaited reissue of the novel that inspired a generation of horse-lovers!

**www.follyfootbooks.co.uk**

9781849391306 £4.99

# Deep Secret

## BERLIE DOHERTY

*Grace put out her hand, almost touching the mirror. Her image did the same.*
*'There's another world in there.'*
*'We could float in and out of it.'*

Deep in a Derbyshire valley live two girls, twins, so alike they seem like one person, even their family can't tell them apart. But tragedy is waiting. When the valley is sold to be flooded for a huge dam, the villagers are forced to leave their homes and the twins' lives are about to change forever. Deep secrets are uncovered and desires, love and grief come to the surface.

'Beautifully written and compulsively readable'
*Independent*

'This is Doherty at her best and her many fans will love it'
*Guardian*

9781849392358  £6.99

# The Unfinished Angel

## SHARON CREECH

*'Peoples are strange!*
*The things they are doing and saying – sometimes they make*
*no sense. Did their brains fall out of their heads?'*

Angel is having an identity crisis when he meets Zola –
a talkative young girl who moves into Angel's tower
high in the Swiss Alps. 'This Zola is a lot bossy,' Angel
thinks. But out of their bickering an unexpected
friendship forms, and their teamwork is about to benefit
the entire village . . .

Sharon Creech won the Carnegie Medal and the
Newbery Medal, and was shortlisted
for the Costa Award. She has sold
over one million copies of her
books worldwide.

'Inventive, sassy and gutsy . . . *The*
*Unfinished Angel* . . . is an endlessly
witty and life-affirming read.'
*Booksellers' Choice,*
*The Bookseller*

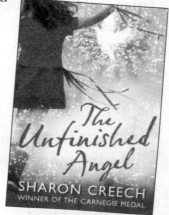

9781849390835 £5.99

# Wuthering Hearts

## Kay Woodward

When Robert arrives in town with his film-star looks and mysterious background, he sends Emily's heart a-flutter. It's almost enough to take her mind off this year's school play . . . miserable old *Wuthering Heights*. Urgh!

But Robert wastes no time in stamping all over Emily's dreams. Is there no escape from his spectacular mean 'n' moodiness? While Emily is trying to make up her mind what she really thinks of the new boy, no one else stands a chance.

It was never this tricky for Cathy and Heathcliff.

*Jane Airhead*, by Kay Woodward: 'A humorous look at teen life and relationships' *Bronteblog*

9781849392990  £5.99